14.00

D0845780

The Separation

Even the book morphs!
Flip the pages
and check it out!

titles in Large-Print Editions:

#31 The Conspiracy

#32 The Separation

#33 The Illusion

#34 The Prophecy

#35 The Proposal

#36 The Mutation

ANIMORPHS ®

The Separation

K.A. Applegate

Gareth Stevens Publishing
A WORLD ALMANAC EDUCATION GROUP COMPANY

For a free color catalog describing Gareth Stevens' list of high-quality books and multimedia programs, call 1-800-542-2595 (USA) or 1-800-461-9120 (Canada). Gareth Stevens Publishing's Fax: (414) 332-3567.

Library of Congress Cataloging-in-Publication Data available upon request from publisher. Fax: (414) 332-3567 for the attention of the Publishing Records Department.

ISBN 0-8368-2759-7

This edition first published in 2000 by
Gareth Stevens Publishing
A World Almanac Education Group Company
330 West Olive Street, Suite 100
Milwaukee, WI 53212 USA

Published by Gareth Stevens, Inc., 330 West Olive Street, Suite 100, Milwaukee, Wisconsin 53212 in large print by arrangement with Scholastic Inc., 555 Broadway, New York, New York 10012.

Printed in the United States of America

1 2 3 4 5 6 7 8 9 04 03 02 01 00

For Michael and Jake

The Separation

CHAPTER 1

My name is Rachel.

Rachel no last name. Rachel no address. Just Rachel.

It's a big, bad world out there, boys and girls. At least my world is. Lions and tigers and bears . . . and those are my friends.

Joke. Sorry, I'm not very good at jokes.

Here's what you need to know: Earth is under attack. Earth is being invaded.

Yes, by aliens.

I know. It sounds like fiction. It sounds like something you'd hear from the crazy lady pushing the shopping cart full of cans down the street. I wish I had a more believable story to tell but all I can do is tell the truth.

1

The truth is that Homo sapiens, humans, me and you, have been targeted by an alien species called Yeerks.

They're a parasitic species. Not predators looking to kill, kill, kill, hovering over our cities and blowing up the Statue of Liberty or whatever. The Yeerks don't want us dead. They don't want our land or our natural resources. They don't want to barbecue our livers.

What they want is us.

They're nothing but gray slugs in their natural state. Helpless. You could put on your Timberlands and stomp a couple thousand of them on the sidewalk.

Except that the Yeerks aren't content to live as slugs. They infest healthy host bodies, they enter the brain, they wrap themselves around the brain and sink into the little crevices. They control the brain. Utterly.

Once they have you, once they've made you a Controller, you don't focus your own eyes, or move your own fingers, or draw your own breath. You are powerless. Like being totally paralyzed, only your eyes are still seeing and your mouth is laughing and your hands are reaching out to choke the life from someone you love. . . .

They're here. They're not E.T. They're not cute. And we, my friends and I, are the only people who know, and just about all that stands between the Yeerks and total world conquest.

Wow. Depressing, huh?

Fortunately, we are not powerless. The Yeerks aren't the only aliens with an interest in Earth. There are the Andalites as well. Night and day. Evil and not evil.

The Andalites may not all be saints, but one of them, a warrior named Elfangor, gave us the Andalite technology that allows us to morph. To acquire the DNA of any animal we touch and then to become that animal.

Morphing: power wrapped up in a nightmare.

And yet, there are times when morphing has certain advantages beyond fighting the Yeerks in their various host bodies.

I was on some rocks, some very wet rocks at the base of a cliff, down by the water. North of town the beaches give way to tumbled rocks and eventually to tall cliffs topped with condos and homes for millionaires.

This particular section of shoreline was public. It was condos to the south, and mansions to the north, but right for about a half mile it was just nature. Big pockmarked boulders and water spraying up and drenching me with each wave, and a chilly breeze raising goose bumps on my bare skin.

3

It was better than being in school. I mean, who doesn't prefer a field trip over another day in the yawn factory?

But it was definitely chilly. Cold once you got soaked. And we were all in shorts and T-shirts, supposedly identifying the "rich and fascinating life of the tidal pool."

Of course what was actually happening was that three kids were investigating life in the tidal pools — including my best friend, Cassie — while most of the boys went leaping about the rocks, and most of the girls moved cautiously in little herds of three or four, and all the teachers and teachers' helpers basically screamed at the boys and chided the girls and occasionally yelled something about echinoderms. Your basic field trip.

I moved away from the others. I don't do the gossip thing very well anymore. Sorry, but, "He said *what*? Oh. My. Gawd! No *way*!" just doesn't do it for me. And leaping around on rocks with boys who are secretly playing superhero in their imaginations, that's not going to work, either.

I do plenty of leaping. Usually there's screaming and bleeding involved. And there's hurting: yourself and others. And afterward there are the nightmares.

There would be more of that real soon. We'd

been informed by our android allies the Chee that the Yeerks were at work on a secret new weapon: an Anti-Morphing Ray. We didn't know enough, yet, to launch an attack. But attack we would. And then there'd be the leaping and screaming and bleeding.

And the nightmares.

Anyway.

I moved steadily away from the others. No one cared. They're glad to see me move on. They don't know why they're relieved when I'm gone, but they are.

I guess I put off bad vibes, as my mom would say.

Once alone it wasn't so bad. I like the sound of waves crashing. And even though it really was cold, I kind of liked the harshness of the landscape. Life down there in the rocks was precarious. You had the ocean, this living thing that encircled the planet, eating away relentlessly at the land, chewing it down, bite by patient bite. And the rocks were nothing but the crumbs that fell from Mother Ocean's mouth.

But there, in those crumbs, in those rocks that would soon be ground into sand, there were hundreds of living things. Entire universes contained in eighteen ounces of seawater cupped in the armpit of a rock.

I knelt down to look at one tidal pool. It went deeper than the others. Down into a crack in the rock, down to darkness.

What tidal pool bogeyman lives down there? I wondered.

There was a starfish sitting glued to the wall of the pool. Might as well have been one of those dead, dried-out things you see in souvenir shops on the boardwalk.

Then he moved. It made me laugh. It was like he'd heard my thoughts and wanted to say, "Hey, I'm not dead yet, kid."

Plop!

I heard the sound.

I made a quick, desperate grab. I missed.

The earring that had fallen from my ear sank quickly out of sight.

"Oh, *man*!" I yelled.

I took off my other earring. I looked at it and groaned again. Yes, it was the hammered-gold hoop my dad had bought me for my last birthday. He'd brought them back from a trip to Portugal. Which meant I wasn't going to be able to replace them at the mall.

I kicked angrily at an outcropping of rock.

This was a bad idea. I was barefoot.

Now I was really mad. Mad that I was on a stupid field trip. Mad that I'd dropped the earring. Mad at my dad for no reason except that I knew he'd expect to see me wearing them on our next weekend visit.

I wanted that earring and I wasn't going to just whine about it. When I get mad, I get determined. When I get mad, I do something. Not always a smart thing.

"You," I said, looking at the starfish. "You could get it back," I said as I took off my outer clothing and stood there in my leotard.

I reached down and touched the starfish and felt it become a part of me.

CHAPTER 2

I stood up. Looked around. Not ten feet away was this guy named Bailey. I don't know if that's his first name or last name.

"What do you want?" I demanded.

"Nothing." He shrugged.

I glared.

He blushed.

"Looking good, Rachel."

"What?"

"That leotard and all. You're looking good."

I was wearing my morphing outfit. It seemed okay for a trip around the rocks.

"Of course I look good," I snapped. "I almost always do. You have something else to say?"

I guess that threw him. He shrugged.

"Looking good," he repeated. "Looking *real* good."

"I think we've been over that," I said. "Now go away."

"You are so stuck-up!"

"That's right, I am. Now you know the difference between good looks and a good personality."

He left. I waited till he was back with a group of his friends. I scanned the other direction along the shoreline. A family with two kids, two little boys. They were coming my way but I'd have time to morph before they got close.

I began to morph.

First I shrank. Smaller and smaller. Puddles and pools rushed up toward me. A shower of spray hit me and all of a sudden it wasn't refreshing, it was scary. The force of the water nearly knocked me off my feet.

Which was easier to do since my feet were disappearing. My thighs grew thick. My arms thickened as well, forming chubby cones.

Arm, arm, leg, leg. And here was the gross part: My head was morphing to become the fifth leg. It turns out starfish don't exactly have heads. They have a mouth more or less in the middle, a bunch of wiggly little feet that look like suckers, and the five big cone legs.

That's about it for a starfish. A cockroach, by comparison, is a model of sophisticated design.

I went blind. Totally. No eyes at all.

It occurred to me to wonder how exactly I expected to find an earring when I couldn't see, but I assumed the starfish would have other compensating senses.

Nope. Not really.

It could feel. It could sort of smell. It could scoot around on its many tiny little feet. If it happened, mostly by accident, to crawl onto something tasty I guess it could eat it. But that was pretty much it for the starfish.

Well, I told myself, *I might be able to feel the earring.*

I motored my many little feet. Down, down, slithering down wet rock.

<Okay, this is stupid. An unfamiliar morph in a hole in the rock. Not your brightest move, Rachel.>

Then my foot — one of them, anyway — touched something thin and hard and round.

Amazing! I had stumbled onto the earring. It took me another ten minutes to get my useless little mouth to grab the earring. I headed back up. At least I hoped it was up.

I climbed up over the lip of the pool, out into relative dryness. I focused my mind on morphing and began to —

WHAM!

Something hit me. Hit me hard.

The starfish didn't have much in the way of pain sensors but I still knew, the starfish knew, deep down, that it was very, very badly hurt.

I tried to make sense of it all. But all I knew for sure was this: I had been able to count to five on my starfish legs.

Now I could only count to two.

I was cut in half!

<Aaaahhhh!> I yelled.

Panic, blind panic hit me.

I was cut in half! I had to die. Had to! There was no way . . .

But I was still alive.

Demorph!

That was it. Yeah. Demorph. Yeah, yeah, change back. Oh, lord! I was chopped in half!

I focused. Focused on the image of myself, my real self.

Demorph, Rachel. Demorph and live!

I began to change.

Eyes! I could see!

Rocks, all around me. But sky above. Blue sky and white, fluffy clouds! I could see!

Tiny little blue eyes sticking out of a starfish leg.

I continued demorphing. I dragged myself up, inch by inch and peeked carefully over the lip of rock.

Half a starfish lay unchanged in the tidal pool. Two legs and a chunk of a third. And an earring.

I caught a glimpse of the family, the two boys. One of them had a pail. And a shiny new steel shovel.

He'd been the one who had cut me.

He'd been the one who'd almost killed me.

Rotten, filthy little brat!

"I'll kill him!" I said. "Kill him! Kill the filthy little creep!" Morph to grizzly bear and tear him apart! No. No. Not the kid. Bailey! His fault. He delayed me, otherwise it would have all worked perfectly.

I stood up.

"Bailey!" I screamed against the crashing waves, shaking my clenched fists in rage. "I'll kill you! I'll kill you! I'll murder you!"

He heard nothing, of course, over the sound of the waves. And that was a good thing.

It occurred to me that killing Bailey was probably an overreaction.

But just the same, it would teach him a lesson.

CHAPTER 3

I finished demorphing. It was a terrifying, hideous experience. But the alternative was even worse. I demorphed in a total, like, panic! I wasn't even thinking, just screaming inside my mind, screaming and begging for it to be over.

I rose from the rocks, so grateful to be fully human, so relieved. I saw the others, far off. I caught a glimpse of a blond girl, running away. I didn't recognize her.

Had she seen me?

The earring! There it was, stuck between my toes. Oh, good. It was a cool earring, really. Not like some of the stuff your parents might buy you. You know parents. Right?

Anyway . . .

13

I ran back to the others, too.

I needed to be with, like, people. I needed to have familiar voices and faces around me.

So scared!

I was shaking. I was going to go on shaking forever.

Was I insane? Why had I done something as reckless as morphing a starfish?

And . . .

And why had I been so mean to Bailey? All he'd wanted to do was compliment me. He just wanted to say he thought I was pretty; why had I been so, like, harsh and stuck-up?

Later I would have to find the time and the right way to apologize. Maybe if I went out on a date with him —

Oh, wait. No. That would hurt Tobias's feelings. I was sure it would.

I was supposed to go flying with Tobias after school. We did that a lot, me and Tobias. Tobias is a *nothlit*. That's an Andalite word for a person who stays in morph past the two-hour limit.

Tobias was trapped now, as a red-tailed hawk.

They are very scary birds.

I mean, he's a boy, really. A very sweet boy. Like Bailey. Only I could kiss Bailey, couldn't I? Yes. I could. It would be nice.

Nice kissing Tobias, too. If he was in human morph.

They were both cute. They were both nice. Sweet. Gentle. Kind. All those good things.

Only, Tobias killed mice and ate them. Which was not all that sweet, really.

Oh, well.

"Are you okay, Rachel?" a girl named Dahlia asked.

"Oh! Does it show?" I asked, pressing my hands against my face.

"Forget it," Dahlia said, looking disgusted. "Why would I try and be nice to you? All I get is sarcasm."

"Oh, Dahlia," I said, reaching out for her. "I'm sorry you feel that way. Really! I want to be friends. I really, really do."

Dahlia made a face. "You know, you were always stuck-up, Rachel, but lately you're just this total, like, witch."

She turned away and I felt hot tears flood my eyes. Why would she say that about me? I was being sincere. I really did want to be friends.

We all walked toward the bus. Boy, was that ever a welcome sight after all I'd been through!

I climbed aboard and got into my seat. My shoes were under the seat. My outer clothing was in my backpack. I pulled a sweater on.

I wish they had seat belts on buses, don't you?

"That's a cute sweater," this girl named Elizabeth said. She was sitting next to me.

15

"Thanks. I got it at Abercrombie? It's, like, on sale? Forty-two fifty marked down to twenty-seven ninety-five."

"No way! Are you going to the mall after school?"

Okay, so I should go straight to meet Tobias after school. That's what I should do. I had promised. Only . . .

But did I want to go be with Tobias? Or did I want to go shopping?

Would Cassie go shopping with me? She didn't like shopping very much. But she might go. I could, like, ask her. But what about Elizabeth? She'd asked me already. Only I didn't really like Elizabeth all that much, and I did like Cassie. Only Cassie might not want to go shopping.

And Tobias! He'd be so sad if I didn't show up.

But if I showed up he'd, like, want me to morph and all, and it was so scary, flying, way up in the air with nothing holding you up — oh my Gawd! I couldn't believe I ever did it!

"So?" Elizabeth asked.

"What?" I asked.

She shrugged. "Forget it."

CHAPTER 4

I hooked up with Tobias at his meadow.

He saw me coming and swept down out of the sky, fierce, wild, a thing of dangerous beauty.

<Hi, Rachel. Hear anything from Jake about the mission?>

"I haven't seen Jake. Don't worry, he'll get word to us if there's killing to be done. Ha! Anti-Morphing Ray! You have to admire the Yeerks: They never stop trying. They never stop trying to take us down! Now, let's fly!"

I began to morph. My bird-of-prey morph is the bald eagle. It's only fitting. Nothing against hawks, but eagles are bigger, more dangerous. I'm sure if Tobias had it to do all over again he'd get trapped as an eagle.

17

The bad part of morphing to eagle is the shrinking. You get smaller. A lot smaller, and your first thought is, *Hey, smaller is weaker and no way I want to be weaker!*

But then you feel your weak, useless human lips harden and push out and out, forming the wicked, yellow, downturned, ripping, tearing eagle beak, and you think, *Hah! Smaller, yes, but not weaker!*

You watch the feather pattern as it draws across your flesh, and feel the strange, distant itching when those patterns become three-dimensional.

Your bones hollow and shrink, your arms twist and rotate, your insides slosh and melt and re-form into inhuman organs.

Your feet, your soft, stubby, awkward human feet melt like wax and then harden into talons.

As wonderful as the eagle's beak is, the talons are the true weapons. So powerful they can grab and hold a young lamb. They can snatch and squeeze and penetrate flesh and organ and skull and brain.

Eyes that can see a flea hopping on a rabbit's back from fifty yards away! Ears that can hear a mouse sneeze! Reflexes like lightning!

A wonderful creature. A natural predator. Raptor! The killer from the sky!

I wondered if I could take Tobias in an air-to-air fight. He was more maneuverable and experienced. But I had the brute power.

Well, another day, maybe. Tobias was a true warrior. The right sort of partner for me. Someone who understood that —

<Ready?> Tobias asked. <Come on, there are some sweet thermals coming up off the freeway today with this sun.>

I flapped my wings. I turned to catch a slight headwind. My wings filled and I soared.

Up and up and up we went. Tobias was right! The thermals off the freeway, the heat boiling up from sunbaked concrete and car engines was like an elevator beneath our wings.

Up and up!

We were gods! We could have flown to the sun! Humans in their cars were puny, flaccid, paltry, limited creatures, far, far beneath us.

A quarter mile up there was a delicious, cool breeze that we used to rocket us forward, zooming over factories and parking lots, over meadows and streams and woods.

Then . . .

Far, far below, so far no human could ever have spotted it, a school of fish, fast and silver, in a stream decorated with garlands of white water.

I spilled air, tucked my wings back, and dove.
The rush!

19

The thrill!

I was an eagle being an eagle. Pure raptor! Pure rapture!

That struck me as a good thought. <Tobias!> I cried. <Pure raptor, pure rapture! Ah HAH!>

<Rachel, what are you doing?>

Down, down, down, so fast the wind was a hurricane over my wings. Then, slow just a bit, use my tail to aim, to change my trajectory as I singled out a single, particular victim.

My eagle's eyes, adapted by nature for seeing through water, filtering out the glare, saw it all: six fish, six trout, all unaware, and one, one I chose, would die!

You! You will never live to chase another fisherman's lure! I have chosen you to die!

I raked my talons forward.

I flared my wings.

A splash!

The sudden, lovely feeling of my talons striking firm, cold flesh.

Strike!

I squeezed and talons sank deep. The fish, only now recognizing its doom, squirmed. *Helpless! I am the eagle! You cannot resist me!*

I fluttered, carrying the spasming creature over to the bank. I landed on a flat rock. I steadied myself with one talon and held my victim with the other.

I looked into his stupid, terrified eyes, and with my razor beak I ripped him open. Scales flew. Fish guts spilled.

I buried my beak, up to the eyes in the cool, squirming flesh. I felt the heart still beating.

I ate the fish, ripping big chunks and gulping them down.

<Rachel! What are you doing? Did you lose control of the morph?>

<What am I doing? I am eating this fish. He's mine! Get back! He's my kill. MY kill!>

I ate the heart. Then, it stopped beating.

CHAPTER 5

"Oh, that outfit is so, like, cute!" I said.

"Uh-huh," Cassie agreed with absolutely no enthusiasm whatsoever.

Cassie is my best friend in the whole world. But she is totally not into clothing or shopping. I mean, I love her, but the girl dresses like someone who should be wearing a tool belt and saying, "Like, can I fix your leaky faucet or whatever?"

Me, I love shopping. I have a talent for it. You know the way Mozart could write music, or Shakespeare could write words? Or the way Will Smith can be all cute? That's how it is with me and shopping.

I had already worked out a plan: the sale at Abercrombie and Fitch, a quick stop at Lady Foot Locker, take the right turn to the department store where they were having a twenty-percent-off sale, swing back past Body Shop, The Limited, and finally top it all off with an Aunt Annie's soft pretzel, no butter but lots of salt.

I'd already figured out what to say to Tobias to apologize. I had an obligation to Tobias, I realized. Yes, an obligation. But shopping was more fun than obligation.

"One third off!" I squealed with delight. "Oh! Do they have my size? It would be so, so cool if they had my size and all. That would be the best!"

"Yeah, that would be right up there with a cure for cancer," Cassie teased.

"You should get one in your size!" I said. "Only, we couldn't ever wear them on the same day, so, like, we'd have to always call each other the night before and check with the other person. And then, if you wanted to wear it, well, if I didn't want to wear it, then okay. Only what if I wanted to wear it the next day? Then it would be like, 'Hey, everyone, Rachel's wearing what Cassie wore yesterday.' So —"

"Rachel?"

"Yes?"

23

"Are you okay?"

"Why do you keep asking me if I'm okay?" I asked.

"Because you're being —"

"Do you think Tobias will be really sad that I didn't go flying with him?" I asked. "I feel bad about that."

"Well, why didn't —"

"Oh, look! Look! No, don't look now! Okay, look! It's the guy from the CD store! He is soooooo cute!"

Suddenly, as I worked my way around the circular sale rack, I brushed into someone.

"Oh, sorry," I said.

"Sorry?"

It was some girl I didn't know. Kind of big. Bigger than me, anyway. And she had, like, this angry look in her eyes. She looked me up and down. Like she didn't like my looks.

It scared me.

I gulped.

"Get out of my way, airhead," she snapped.

Cassie jumped forward and put her hand on my arm. "Rachel, let it go."

The girl guffawed. "Yeah, Rachel, let it go. Get out of my way before I kick your skinny, preppy, mall-crawling, bubblehead, blond butt."

"Rachel," Cassie warned, "let it go. You don't need to go postal over this."

I felt the tears start. I bit my lip.

"S-s-s-sorry," I said to the mean, mean girl.

I turned and ran away. I buried my face in my hands and ran.

"What the . . ." Cassie said.

"You, too, Farm Girl," I heard the mean girl say to Cassie.

I stopped running when I found a bench outside Baby Gap. I just, like, sat there, all collapsed, trying to get hold of myself.

Cassie came running up. She's my best friend. So I knew she'd talk to me and be nice and make me feel better.

I looked up at her through blurry tears.

She stood with hands on hips and a shocked expression on her face and looked down at me.

"Okay," she said, "what have you done with Rachel?"

CHAPTER 6

I hate the mall. I don't know why I ever thought I liked it. Must be one of those things where you just suddenly wake up one day, the scales fall from your eyes, and you behold The Truth: The mall sucks.

I mean, if you ever want to really experience contempt for your fellow human beings, go to the mall. They moo along like cattle, little knots of them, little gaggles of them. Like sheep!

Tired-looking, pasty-faced mommies busily crushing the wild free spirits of their children; galumphing teen boys with idiot expressions covered by acne pustules; high-heeled trophy wives with their squat, bald, fireplug husbands in tow.

What a hideous spectacle. And all for what?

To buy, buy, buy! Shopping: sport of the brain-dead.

But what was I going to do? I had to do something with my clothing situation. I mean it was pathetic! After flying with Tobias, and after he got all weird, I headed home. I'd left my clothes on the bus after I ditched the stupid field trip. Anyway, I get home, and what do I find in my closet? Girl clothes!

Yeah, yeah, I am a girl. But I mean that all of my clothing was so squeaky clean, so preppy, so "good girl."

I'd never really thought about it before. I mean, I bought the stupid clothes, all right? But they chewed!

I needed something with a little more of an edge, man. I needed some leather, yeah, some black leather. That was it. Leather.

I tried to think of what to do. I mean, I guess I knew I'd have to go to the mall, but it was complicated. First I didn't know how to get there. Then, once I was there, I didn't know where to go. Too many shops. I tried to think about it, you know, focus and all, but it was just confusing.

Confusing because it was so stupid! That's why. Because it was stupid!

I shoved past this obnoxious couple that was getting all goo-goo because their kid was walking. He was like two. Big deal, he could walk.

"Hey! Watch it, please!"

"You watch it, old man," I replied politely.

"My son is trying to walk," the woman said.

"Yeah, and with your DNA in him that'll probably be his highest accomplishment," I said tolerantly.

I brushed past. I spotted Cassie up ahead and slowed up. Didn't need her, right then. Cassie's all right, but man, she can complicate the simplest thing. You know? I mean, life is pretty simple, right? The strong eat the weak. That's about it. No complications.

Cassie was running toward Baby Gap. Great, she'd probably meet up with the proud mommy and daddy and the staggering, drooling baby.

I cut into Williams-Sonoma, the kitchen store, to avoid having Cassie see me. Don't know why, just didn't want to hook up with her right then.

So anyway, I go into Williams-Sonoma, and what do I see? Knives! So many knives! A rack of them with plastic over it, plus a counter with a bunch of them in knife blocks.

Well, I like knives. How can you not like knives?

"Aww, it's the crybaby," someone said. Some girl.

I pushed past her.

She grabbed my arm. This was a mistake.

I grinned at her. "Back off, you hideous, pu-trid, diseased-looking lump of lard," I said.

I was being nice. I was giving her a chance.

"What are you gonna do, little J. Crew girl? Bust out in tears a —"

My right hand shot toward her throat. She jumped back. I lashed out with my left foot and caught her hard on the shin.

She yelled.

A good sound.

I plowed into her, shoulder down, and slammed her back against the knife rack.

The twelve-inch chef's knife was in my hand. So easy to plunge it into her heart.

But you know, I kind of liked this girl. She re-minded me of me.

I grabbed a handful of her sweatshirt.

Thunk!

I buried the chef's knife in her sweatshirt. The knife quivered in the wood counter. She was pinned.

She was scared, too.

I grabbed more sweatshirt and . . .

Thunk!

The boning knife went in.

Thunk!

Bread knife.

Thunk!

Seven-inch utility knife.

Naturally, she was screaming during all this. "Ahhhh! Ahhhh! Ahhhh!"

I grabbed the cleaver. I held it high in the air, like I was gonna slam it down on her head.

Then, I laughed. I pinched her cheek and tugged back and forth while she shook and quivered.

"I like you," I said. "I really do. We could be friends. But watch who you pick your fights with."

I walked away, sliding past the security guards who were rushing in.

Maybe the mall isn't so bad after all.

CHAPTER 7

Cassie's barn. I'd been there a hundred times. But now it seemed different. Scary.

I mean it's like, full of, like, animals. Wild animals. Geese. Raccoons. Foxes. Squirrels.

Okay, I know squirrels aren't scary, but sometimes they have rabies.

It's kind of dark inside. There are lights on, but there are shadows, too. Deep shadows. Especially at night. Which it wasn't. It was day. Late afternoon. Or is it evening? When does afternoon end and evening begin? I mean, is there like a certain time when . . .

Anyway, it was like day, okay? But inside it was still dark and all. I could see the animals in their cages. Mostly sick or injured because after all it is the Wildlife Rehabilitation Clinic. So, duh, they would be sick or injured to be in a clinic, right?

Duh, Rachel.

What was I saying?

Oh, yes, the animals. Well, there were a lot of them, in cages.

But just as scary was the fact that the others were there, too. The Animorphs.

I mean, I am an Animorph, right? I have the morphing power that Elfangor gave us all. And I have turned into, like, lots of animals. Although now I can't believe I ever did that.

Jake was there. He's my cousin. He's cute. Kind of big. I mean, if we weren't cousins . . .

And Marco was there, too. He's cute, too, in a different way. I would probably go out with him if he asked me.

And Tobias, of course. He was up in the rafters fluffing up his wings. He's cute when he's human.

And Ax.

Ax is not cute. Ax is very, very strange. I mean he's, like, not human? He's, like, an alien. Imagine if you had this big, mostly blue deer, and you grafted a long scorpion tail on one end and a human-looking upper body on the other end. Only the head didn't have a mouth at all and it had an extra set of eyes on stalks? Stalks that can, like, move? So his eyes can look in any direction?

Major creepy.

"We have a problem," Cassie said, looking at me.

"We do?" I said.

"Jake, we were at the mall," Cassie said. "Some girl shoved Rachel and —"

"Oh, man, what did you do, Rachel?" Jake asked. "You have to learn to restrain your —"

"She cried," Cassie said.

"What?"

"She cried. And ran away. And cried."

Everyone stared at me.

"Who cried?" Marco demanded, looking confused.

"Rachel."

"Rachel cried?" Marco asked. "You mean a little wetness, like maybe something was in her eye?"

"I mean like 'Boo hoo, that girl was so mean,'" Cassie clarified.

"No," Marco said.

"Yes."

"No. No. The sun does not rise in the west, the Chicago Cubs don't win the World Series, Scully never, ever believes Mulder, and Rachel does not cry. These are the things I know."

"Boo. Hoo."

"You're jerking us around, Cassie," Marco said.

"I have proof," Cassie said.

"Okay," Jake said skeptically.

Cassie looked at me. "Rachel? Tell me what you said to me about Marco on our way over here."

"What?"

"What you said to me on the bus about Marco."

"You mean that he was like, funny?"

"Oh my . . ." Jake whispered.

"Rachel," Cassie pressed, "what do you think of Marco's looks?"

I shrugged. I smiled. "He's, like, cute, all right?"

Marco sat down very suddenly. On the hay-strewn floor.

Jake looked pale.

<This is unusual,> Ax said in thought-speak.

"She's uptalking," Marco said, shaken. "She said I was cute. She . . . she smiled. At me."

"Ax," Jake said and shot the Andalite a look. FWAPP!

Faster than the human eye could see, Ax's tail whipped forward, over his head. The long, scythe blade stopped a millimeter from my throat.

"Yeerk," Marco said. "Has to be. They've infested her."

"No, no, no," Cassie said. "If she was a Controller she'd sound exactly like Rachel. This is something different. A breakdown, maybe."

<She was weird with me, too,> Tobias said. <But in a different way. She was brutal, violent. In eagle morph she killed and ate a fish. She ate it while it was still living.>

Ax kept his blade against my throat. I would have fainted except that falling down could have been, like, fatal.

So I kept my quivering knees as firm as I could. But nothing would stop the tears rolling down my cheeks.

"Look!" Marco cried, like he'd just spotted the Holy Grail sitting on top of the Golden Fleece. "Tears!"

"What on Earth is —" Jake started to say.

But then the door of the barn burst open.

"All right! What's the mission, when do we start, and how many Yeerks do we get to kill today? I am hungry for some wild butt-kicking! Hah HAH!"

CHAPTER 8

Nice Rachel

I stared.

She stared.

She was me. I was her.

"There're two of them!" Jake said.

<They appear to be identical,> Ax said.

"Cool!" Marco said, climbing to his feet. "Now Tobias can have one and I can have the oth — AAAAHHHH!"

I . . . I mean *she* . . . somersaulted.

She leaped, landed on her hands, flew through the air, and landed, feetfirst, against Marco's chest.

Marco landed very hard on his back. Rachel was astride him, squatting on his chest. Her knees pinned his arms. She reached behind his head and grabbed a handful of his dark hair.

The other hand was balled into a fist, quivering, about a foot away from Marco's face.

"What did you say?" Rachel whispered.

"Not one single thing," Marco said. "Me? I said nothing."

Rachel . . . I mean, the other Rachel, of course, rolled off him and laughed. It was a big, hearty, HAH HAH HAH laugh.

Ax withdrew the blade from my throat. I collapsed in a heap.

She stood over me. "Hey. You look like me."

I nodded, lip quivering.

"What's going on here?" she demanded loudly.

<That seems to be the question at hand,> Ax said mildly.

"The Drode? One of his tricks?" Jake demanded.

Cassie shrugged.

They kept staring. At me. At *her*. Back at me. It was like being an animal in a zoo.

And I kept staring, too. At her. For one thing, she was dressed totally differently from me. She was so, like, L.L. Bean meets Timberland by way of a Harley-Davidson rally. Not at all my look.

Although, when I thought about it, my look could use some freshening up. I mean, what was with all the pants and jeans? Why shouldn't I wear dresses? I have great legs. I can wear dresses and look good. The shorter lengths, the longer lengths, like, you know, with a slit or whatever? Why shouldn't I try the waif look, I mean I can be a waif. I can do the slinky dresses with, like, the big —

"Ow!"

Someone was knocking on my head. It was *her*.

She rapped my skull with her knuckles. "Hey! Hey! You awake in there? I asked you a question. Who are you? And what are you doing with my body?"

Marco fidgeted. "Um, I have a body joke here, but I can't tell it unless Ax promises to protect me."

"Shut up," Mean Rachel snapped. "Don't make me kill you. Now, you, little pansy girl, you have about three seconds to tell us —"

"Don't threaten," Jake said with unmistakable authority.

Mean Rachel forgot me in a flash. She rounded on Jake. "Don't get in my way, Jake."

"Don't push it, Rachel."

"Are you threatening me?" she nearly screamed. "Come on! You think you can tell me what to do? Let's go, right now. You and me. Just keep our pet Andalite here out of the fight. You and me, we'll see who's giving orders around here after I give you the butt-kicking you're begging for."

The possible fight was interrupted at this point by the arrival of Erek King. He's a Chee. Meaning that he's, like, this Android? Only he uses holograms to look like this normal boy.

I don't think he's cute because, you know, it's bad enough being attracted to a guy who's a bird of prey, right? Getting into androids is maybe going a little far.

Although, when you realize Erek is really like thousands of years old, so he's totally mature and all —

Anyway.

Erek walked in. Looking like a boy. Looking like a boy with a very odd expression on his face.

"Um . . ." he said. "Um . . . is it just me, or are there really two Rachels here?"

"We're filming a Doublemint gum commercial later," Marco said, then cringed lest Mean Rachel go all psycho-gymnast on him again.

"Yeah, we have two Rachels," Jake said.

"Okay. Any particular reason?" Erek asked.

"It wasn't exactly deliberate," Cassie explained.

<They appear to be identical,> Ax said. <Except that one is passive and easily frightened, and the other is —>

"Excitable?" Marco suggested.

<— violent and aggressive,> Ax concluded.

Erek nodded. "Dr. Jekyll and Mr. Hyde?"

"Well, it's sure not Mary Kate and Ashley," Marco said.

<So it was *you* who went flying with me, today,> Tobias said.

"Who? Me?" I asked.

<No. The other one,> Tobias said.

"Mean Rachel," Marco suggested. "Mean Rachel and Nice Rachel?"

"Mighty Rachel, hah HAH!" Mean Rachel said. "Mighty Rachel, and . . . and . . . Wimp Rachel! Yeah, that's it, blondie."

I didn't exactly want to be known as "Wimp Rachel." But I didn't want Mean Rachel to try and pound my face in, either.

"This is nuts," Cassie said.

"I can't stay long," Erek said, unable to stop looking from me to Mean Rachel and back again. "I just came to update you guys on the mission."

"To the Yeerk pool!" Mean Rachel crowed. "Let's get some flamethrowers!"

"I gotta stop hanging around with you people," Erek said. "You people are just plain strange."

CHAPTER 9

Mean Rachel

"It's called the Buyers Research Institute. They test consumer products and have a magazine," Erek explained. "The Yeerks just recently bought it to use as a front. Also, they hope to use the BRI's consumer ratings to help some of their other companies. So we —"

"We go in, hard and fast," I said. "Forget subtlety and concealment, we go in, all guns blazing, battle morphs, maximum shock value. Anything gets in our way we kill it!"

"Rachel?" Jake said.

"What?"

"What?"

"*Mean* Rachel," he clarified.

"What?" I asked.

41

"Why don't we let Erek finish before we decide how to deal with this. Erek?"

The android nodded his human head. It was such a pity. The Chee were powerful beyond human imagining, but programmed for nonviolence. We'd freed Erek from that programming once and man, he had carried out gross and total mayhem! It was beautiful! Of course, now he was back in his old Gandhi-Martin-Luther-King-Give-Peace-a-Chance mode.

Pity.

"Well, as you know," Erek continued, "we believe the Anti-Morphing Ray is a real threat to all of you. If it works it would destroy the morphing field and cause a person in morph to demorph."

"If it works," Wuss Rachel said. "Probably it won't even work, so we have nothing to worry about."

"Shut up," I snapped.

"The problem you have is that preliminary testing is about to begin tonight," Erek said. "Just computer simulations and so on, but it may encourage the Yeerks. You should stop them before it gets that far. Which means moving right away. Tonight."

"Okay, Erek, thanks. We'll take it from here," Jake said.

Erek left. Gratefully, I think.

<I think we need to figure this situation out,>

Tobias said. <I mean, we need to go after this Anti-Morphing Ray but first we need to figure out what the deal is with two Rachels.>

I leered at him. "You're as bad as Marco. You want us both. Hah HAH! I'll be more than enough for you, Tobias; you won't be needing the wimp, here."

<That wasn't exactly what —>

"Okay, Rachel . . . both of you . . . tell us what you did today," Jake said.

"School, field trip, here, big deal, let's go squash some slugs!" I said.

"Well, first I woke up, then I took a shower, then —"

"Field trip," Cassie interrupted. "What happened on the field trip?"

"You were there," I said. "Don't waste my time with stupid questions."

"I was there, but not with you," Cassie said.

"I remember it was chilly," my idiot twin said. "I had, like, goose bumps?"

"I used to read those books," Marco said.

<Rachel had books in response to cold?> Ax asked.

"Focus, can we please focus, here?" Jake said.

"I dropped my earring in a tidal pool!" Nitwit Rachel said suddenly, sounding as excited as if she'd just answered correctly to Final Jeopardy.

"Stupid earring," I said.

"My favorite earrings! My dad gave them to me."

"Guilt gift," I sneered.

"It was sweet."

"It was a payoff for missing our visit that weekend."

"He was busy!"

"Right."

"You are horrible!"

"And you're a pinhead."

"Dr. Jekyll? Ms. Hyde?" Cassie interrupted. "Can we move on?"

"I couldn't reach the earring, it fell down in this, like, crack?"

"In this, *like*, crack? Crack, question mark? Was it a crack or wasn't it? If it was a crack then say 'it fell in a crack!' No 'like.' No question mark. Crack, crack, CRACK!"

I couldn't believe this bimbo.

"I wanted it back because I thought my dad would be sad if he thought —"

"Oh, someone just gag me," I snapped. "The earring was in a crack. I morphed this starfish to go in after it."

<You morphed a starfish?> Tobias asked.

"Did you go deaf?" I asked him. Sweetly. "Pay attention, this is tough enough with her babbling."

"And then, oooh, it was horrible! Horrible!"

"Huh?" I asked.

"Someone, something . . . the pain! I was so scared! I was, like, cut in, like, half?"

"Some rotten little monster of a kid," I yelled, renewed in my rage at the memory. "I should have killed him! I should have morphed to grizzly and gone after him!"

"Back up," Cassie said. "You morphed to starfish and some kid chopped you in half."

I grabbed Cassie's arm. "Hey, why are you talking to the wimp? Talk to me. Talk to ME!"

"Nice Rachel? Did you demorph right away?" Cassie pressed.

"No, I was too scared! I mean, like —"

"Mean Rachel, how about you?"

"Of course I demorphed right away. What was I going to do, try and destroy Bailey as a freaking starfish?"

<Bailey?> Ax asked.

Jake shrugged. "Don't ask *me*."

"Oh, man," Cassie said.

<What?> Tobias asked her.

"Starfish. I mean, at one level it was lucky. She could have been killed."

"Cassie," Jake said in his I'm-losing-patience-but-still-trying-to-be-polite voice. "Tell us what you know."

"Starfish. They regenerate. You can chop off a leg and they can grow a new one. Somehow when that starfish was chopped in half, the starfish's regenerative powers created the possibility of two separate Rachels. One in each half."

<But, somehow the two halves were unequal, subtly different,> Ax said. <This is a very interesting phenomenon.>

"Interesting?" Marco shrilled. "It's bizarre! It's weird. It's wacko, creepy, horrific, incredible, absurd, and totally, totally, I mean *totally* insane. But also, kind of cool."

"Wait a minute!" I cried. "The shrimp-boy is right! I should have seen the possibilities, but I'm getting confused. The wimp here can attend school and keep the 'rents happy and I can spend a hundred percent of my time in fierce battle against the Yeerks! I'll annihilate them! I'll crush them! They won't know what hit 'em. It will be full-time Rachel, on the loose!"

"Good grief," Jake muttered. "Okay, here's the deal: Nice Rachel, you sit this mission out. Go home. Stay home. And Mean Rachel?"

"Yes?" I asked, filled with excitement.

"You do the same. Home. Quiet. Don't hurt anyone. We'll handle BRI and the AMR without you. Either of you."

Naturally, I objected. But Jake wouldn't give.

"I'll kill you!" I screamed at him. "I'll kill you all!"

They left me anyway.

CHAPTER 10

Nice Rachel

Mean Rachel snuck in the house morphed as a cockroach, then demorphed right in front of me.

I couldn't watch. I pressed my hands over my eyes. It was so awful!

I mean, okay, I know that I have morphed roaches myself. It's not like I'm dumb or anything. I have the same memories as Mean Rachel. So, like, I know all the stuff I've done in the past, right?

But now it just seems so far away. Like some old nightmare. It's still scary, right, but it's like, far away.

Besides, that wasn't my real problem now.

"GET OFF MY BED!"

I jumped. I jumped and slipped off the edge of the bed and landed on my butt on the floor. I almost dropped Bobo Bear.

"But . . ." I said.

"Two of us and only one bed, you do the math," Mean Rachel said.

"W-w-we could sh-sh-share."

"We c-c-could sh-sha-share?" she mocked me. "You were never a part of me. Never! I can't believe you and I were ever inside the same person. You make me want to vomit! I should . . ."

She didn't say what she should do. I didn't want to think about it.

"Rachel?"

A voice through the door. My little sister, Jordan.

"What!?" Mean Rachel roared.

"What?" I asked.

"Are you . . . are you talking to yourself in there?" Jordan asked.

"Yeah, you got a problem with that?" Mean Rachel yelled.

"No," came the muffled response. "I just like to keep track of your level of insanity."

Mean Rachel lay there quivering with suppressed energy. "I need to do something!"

"W-w-what?"

She shot a suspicious look at me. "Something. I'll think of something. Just have to focus."

"I . . . I mean, I, you know, I'm kind of having a hard time focusing, too," I said.

"I'm not having trouble focusing, you moron. I can focus. I'm not like you. It's just . . . I mean, you can't know the future, right? Put a Yeerk here, put a bunch of Hork-Bajir in front of me, I'll focus! I'll focus them to death!"

I started to say something to her, only, what was it? Something. Or not. Things just seemed to evaporate right out of my brain.

So I said, "The others are probably starting on the mission. I hope they're —"

"That's it!" Mean Rachel cried.

"What's it?"

"The mission! I'm going on the mission!" Mean Rachel glared at me with hatred in her eyes. "Don't look at me, I don't want you busting out in tears. I'm going to morph and then I'm outta here."

"But Jake said —"

"Hey, Jake isn't the boss of me," Mean Rachel snapped. "He may not be the boss of anything much longer. The powerful rule over the weak. The strong survive, honey pie. And I am the strong!"

I turned my back on her and hugged Bobo Bear. I heard the window slide up. Then, I put my hands over my ears to block out the faint sounds of grinding bones and liquefying flesh.

<And don't get back up on that bed,> she said. <I'll know! If you get back on that bed I'll put you in the hospital! I'll break both your arms. Then see how well you can hug B-B-Bobo B-B-Bear.>

I didn't look up until I was totally, totally sure she was gone.

I had a plan. I was going to call my dad. But when should I call him? Now? Later? Now?

What? What was I thinking about?

Dad! Call Dad! I had to write it down fast before I forgot again. "Call Daddy," I said as I carefully wrote it down.

I went to the phone. I picked it up, trembling, careful not to touch the bed.

I was trapped in a nightmare. And it wasn't just this being split-in-two thing. I had been trapped in a nightmare since that awful night when we first ran into Elfangor and he, like, messed up our lives and all.

Secrets! Nothing but secrets!

Nightmares and horrors!

And the worst horror of all was seeing what had grown inside of me like some kind of cancerous tumor. Mean Rachel was getting stronger with each passing month of my life as an Animorph. Pretty soon she would have become all of me and there'd have been nothing left of *me*!

It had to end! I didn't care if the strong survived and the weak perished, I wanted to survive anyway!

I blinked away the tears. What was I doing? Something. I saw the note. Oh yeah.

I dialed my dad's phone number.

CHAPTER 11

Mean Rachel

The night and owl morph.

It was like being some kind of a god!

I could see what no one else saw. I could hear what no one else heard. I flew, silent as the grave, through early night.

Over the rooftops! Skimming the chimney tops. Flitting through the highest branches of the highest trees. The bright, square windows below me, the pale streetlights, the searching headlights of the cars were all unnecessary. I needed nothing but the faintest glimmer of light to see clearly. I could read a book from a hundred feet away by the light of a single, flickering candle.

Great horned owl. The night killer of the skies.

I saw it all from up there. The worker-drones getting home late from their pathetic jobs; the mommies making din-din for their yowling, savage little children; the TV screens flickering with the news of the world.

Hah! News? I had news for the world: Rachel was on the loose! Rachel was unrestrained! Look out, world, Rachel was on the wing, talons ready!

Ah HAH!

Buyers Research Institute. Yeah. Had to go there, that's where the mission was. And when I got there? I'd . . . I'd . . . I'd figure something out. That's what I'd do. Just get there. That's all that mattered.

You don't need a plan, Rachel, I told myself. *The Great and Powerful Rachel does not need a stupid plan.* No, no. The Mighty Rachel would arrive and then, that would be it! Let the battle begin. Let those fools — my friends — see how weak they were without me.

Maybe if one of them were torn apart by Hork-Bajir that would teach them a lesson!

Then I spotted the cat. The silent predator was stalking a mouse in its own backyard.

Ah, yes, friend cat. A worthy adversary. He would give me a fight to tune me up and get my blood boiling for the wild massacre ahead!

53

I tilted my tail and reconfigured my wings.

Friend Tabby would not even hear my approach. Kitty Kitty wouldn't know what hit him!

Down, down, with talons spread wide. I would hit the cat in the neck from behind. One talon would close over his head and I would squeeze, squeeze till the talon broke through the skull and —

The cat jumped sideways, quick as lightning.

I saw my error too late! It was the mouse. He'd been facing me. He'd seen my shadow as I passed beneath the streetlight. His shocked, upward gaze had alerted the cat!

I swished helplessly by.

Oh! The unfairness of it! The cat was mine, mine. MINE!

Rage boiled up within me. I wanted that kill! I wanted that kill! I needed that kill! I needed to feel my talons breaking bone and squishing brain and . . .

I couldn't think. Couldn't focus. Madness. Like blood in my eyes. The rage, it was like someone had exploded a hand grenade in my stomach. Like the explosion couldn't get out but was all contained inside me.

My wings . . . they wouldn't work. I . . . couldn't focus. . . . Mine, mine, MINE! My kill! My kill! My kill!

I landed hard on a patch of grass beside the

road. Cars zipped by, swirling me with their backwash.

I lay there, on my back, feathers dampened by the grass, and kicked my bird legs and flapped my bird wings and threw my head back and forth and screamed.

Screamed and screamed and screamed and still the volcano inside me would not die down.

It seemed like forever. It was a fever. An illness. A tidal wave of emotion that had rolled over me. How long it lasted, I don't know. A long time, it seemed to me. Then, at last, it ebbed.

It ebbed, leaving behind a shaky, uncertain feeling.

Fear?

Yes. Fear.

Fear of myself.

And yet, the hunger was not lessened in any way. I had missed this kill. I wouldn't miss the next.

I flew toward the Buyers Research Institute.

CHAPTER 12

Mean Rachel

Buyers Research Institute. The people who tell you which vacuum cleaner to buy and which coffee tastes best.

You are one sad, tired, burned-out specimen of humanity if you need someone to tell you which vacuum to buy. I mean, buy the vacuum, if it doesn't work go back and get the salesman and kick his butt! Where's the big mystery there?

That's how I'd do it, anyway.

It was three stories high. Rectangular. One of those big, modern, nothing buildings you see in industrial parks or by the side of the highway.

Lights were on in only a small handful of the

offices, and no one was in those. I could see that clearly. The building looked empty. And with my predator's eyes I realized something else: There was a missing floor.

They supposedly did all kinds of testing and stuff, but all I was seeing were offices with cluttered desks and computer monitors endlessly playing their Mystify Your Mind screen savers.

Below ground. That must be where the testing was done. Yeah, now that I looked I could see a large truck bay cut deep enough to open into a sublevel.

I floated almost effortlessly past the top floor of windows. Jake and the others must already be inside. Fine. When the stuff hit the fan I'd be —

BBBBBRRRRRRRRRIIIINNNNNGGGGG!

The sound was magnified to my sensitive owl ears. An alarm!

BBBBBRRRRRRRRRIIIINNNNNGGGGG!

It was like the class bell times ten. Definite alarm!

My friends needed help. Yeerks needed killing.

<Cool!>

But how to get into the building? No time for slow infiltration. I needed something direct.

The truck bay.

I whipped my wings and swung around above

the truck bay. It was a long, fairly steep ramp that went from the rear parking area of the building straight down to a loading dock.

The loading dock was a concrete pier protected by two big rubber buffers. The opening itself was a retractable steel door.

The door was too much even for my grizzly morph. No other way in, not that I could see.

Then, I spotted the truck. It was a car carrier. You know, one of those trucks where they precariously pile five or six new cars on the ramped trailer?

Must be new car models coming to be tested, I thought.

The truck was parked at the edge of the parking lot. There was a faint light from inside the cab. The driver was probably inside catching a nap. Maybe he showed up too late for his scheduled drop-off; I didn't know, didn't care. I just cared that the key was probably in that truck.

BBBBBRRRRRRRRIIIINNNNNGGGGG!

The ringing wasn't stopping! I was probably missing half the slaughter!

I landed behind the truck. I demorphed as fast as I could, then morphed again.

A few seconds later the driver was awakened when I removed the door of his truck.

"Aaaaahhhhh! Aaaahhhhh!" he said.

He was scared, good and scared, and it made

me laugh. So I let him live. I reached in with massive grizzly paws and yanked him out, kicking and screaming and wetting himself.

Then, I climbed into the cab.

"Hey! Hey! You can't steal my rig!" he yelled.

I stomped on the clutch. I rammed the gearshift forward. I didn't exactly know how to drive a truck, but to my surprise it lurched forward when I let go of the clutch.

WHAM!

I hit some stupid Volkswagen. It didn't slow me down too much.

The truck steered badly. And holding the wheel wasn't easy with my ham-sized paws. But the big rig turned and slowly, slowly gained speed.

Turned . . . turned . . . and now, straightened out as I aimed the tons of steel down the ramp!

<Ah HAAAAHHHHH!> I screamed in pure joy as the truck plunged forward and down.

Faster . . . faster . . .

WHAAAAMMMMM!

The truck stopped very suddenly against the concrete pier.

TWANNNG!

The safety chain holding the foremost car in place snapped.

The car flew off the front end of the truck, right over the cab, into the steel door, through the steel door, wrapping the hinged metal around itself and veering off to one side.

A second car flew right behind it but no longer found a door in its way.

The steering wheel had sledgehammered my chest on impact. My weight shattered the wheel and without remembering how, exactly, I found myself head and shoulders through the windshield.

I was winded, bruised, and cut. But it takes more than a little truck accident to kill a grizzly bear.

The door of the truck bay was open.

I snatched up the key chain, worked my way through the rest of the windshield, and climbed clumsily over the big Peterbilt engine.

I landed hard on a concrete floor. But I was inside! I was a grizzly bear!

And I had the second car that had flown off the end of the truck. A Mercedes convertible.

Silver metallic.

Very cool.

CHAPTER 13

Nice Rachel

"Daddy?"

"Hi, honey!"

I clutched the phone with one hand and Bobo Bear with the other.

"Daddy?"

"Of course, who else would it be? Is something the matter?"

"Oh, Daddy, everything is the matter!"

"That sounds serious."

"It is, it is!"

"Are you okay?"

"Can you tell?" My dad's a TV reporter. He has very good instincts.

"Tell what?"

61

"Rachel, I'm asking if you're okay. You don't sound like yourself."

"I don't? But I am. Me, I mean. I am me. Maybe . . . I mean maybe I'm a little different or, like, you know, not a hundred percent the same."

"Is it drugs? Sweetheart, you know you can tell me. Are you on drugs?"

"Um, I took two Motrin for my headache . . . Oh! You mean like drug drugs? No, of course not!"

He sounded relieved. "Thank God! That's all I need. I mean, all you need. You know what I mean. Just did a three-part story on drug use among young teens, I mean, very in-depth with some great interviews and some killer footage. Great stuff! And they make me chop it down to a minute thirty. A minute thirty!"

"Um, Daddy? This is, like, about me, okay?"

"Of course, of course. How are you?"

I felt my lip quiver. "Not very good."

"Have you talked to your mom? She's pretty good with this kind of stuff."

"What kind of stuff?"

"Oh . . . well . . . I guess, boy stuff? Does it involve boys?"

"Yes, yes, it does! How did you guess? Actually three boys. I mean, four if you count this one guy who is like, you know, okay, not exactly a *boy*, if you know what I mean."

"A man!" he shrieked in my ear. "A man? You're going out with a man? Are you seeing a college kid?"

"No, Daddy. Duh! That's not what I meant, it's just that he's . . . foreign."

"An alien?"

I almost choked Bobo Bear. I lowered my voice to a whisper. "How did you know?"

"Well, honey, it's not that big a deal. I mean, my cleaning lady is an alien and she does a great job."

I had to think about that for a minute.

"She's from Ukraine," he said.

"Oh! That kind of alien!"

"Yeah. Ukraine. It used to be part of the old Soviet Union."

I nodded. "We learned about that in school. The old Soviet Union. Although I don't know why anyone would name their country 'the Old' anything. I mean, did it used to be the new Soviet Union and then, after a long time they figured, 'Well, we can't exactly call it "new" anymore, can we?'"

"Uh-huh. Look, Rachel? You said something was bothering you. A boy?"

"Who?"

"I don't know who." He sounded annoyed.

"I just can't keep it all bottled up inside anymore!"

"Keep what bottled up inside?"

"Shh! I can't say over the phone. They could be listening and Jake would go totally, totally nuts!"

"Jake? You're going out with Jake? As in Jake, your cousin?"

I laughed. "Silly! You always make me feel better."

"Ooookay."

"Come soon, okay? Can you come tomorrow? I have to talk to you. It's about . . . about what you said before."

"Drugs?"

"No, your . . ." I searched for a way to tell him without committing the unpardonable sin of blurting it over the phone. "Your cleaning lady," I said, trying to say it in a way so he'd know it wasn't really, exactly about his cleaning lady. "It's about, you know. What you said about her."

"That she's from Ukraine?"

He got it! The code was working. "Exactly. It's about Ukraine."

Long pause. "I'll be there tomorrow."

He hung up. I hung up. I felt better. Tomorrow I would tell him everything. The Yeerks, the Animorphs, the whole thing about Tobias being a hawk and also me kind of liking him. And about there being two of me.

He would know what to do.

I heard the phone ring but by then I was already heading downstairs. My mom picked it up. I could hear her voice, sounding icy.

"No, she is not on drugs. I would know! Unlike certain people, I see her every day."

CHAPTER 14

Mean Rachel

I couldn't find the right key to start the silver Mercedes. But I made a cool discovery: If you jab about six inches of bear claw into the key slot, it'll work!

I flattened the driver's seat. I jammed one big foot down on the accelerator, and I was off!

Vrrrrooom!

It was just what I thought: The basement level was one big, huge testing facility. It was like a warehouse, kind of. A cement floor with broad aisles, with clusters of machinery to the left and the right. The basement level extended much farther in every direction than the upper levels had.

Some of the tests seemed to be automated. Machines were busily carrying them out without human supervision. Or at least there were no humans around that I could see.

Then again, your average cowardly human would tend to run away if he saw a grizzly bear driving a convertible toward him. I wouldn't run away, of course, but then I'm not exactly average.

I roared along past machines that were automatically twisting the knobs of stereos; past a table that held twenty or thirty hair dryers in place as they blew; past twin lines of La-Z-Boys being jerked out and back, out and back, like they were inhabited by a brigade of invisible, hyperactive fathers. One of the recliners was already broken. A steel shank kept jerking out through the footstool with each movement.

The first alarm had stopped now. A second, different alarm had taken over.

Brr-REEEET! Brr-REEEET! Brr-REEEET!

I could hear it quite well over the gentle hum of the Mercedes engine.

To my left I spotted a test involving blue jeans. About two dozen pairs were mounted on leg-shaped steel prongs that appeared to be stretching them. Two dozen pairs, all of them feet upward.

I slammed on the brakes and the car squealed down the slick cement.

I peered, looking for my favorite brand. But my grizzly bear eyes were too weak to make out labels.

I took off again and suddenly a troop of Hork-Bajir trotted right across my path. There were eight. Obviously in a hurry. No doubt in pursuit of my friends.

I kept my foot on the accelerator. The last Hork-Bajir spotted me bearing down on him. He yelled something and leaped aside.

Hah! Not likely!

I twisted the wheel. I was on two wheels! I was so far over on one side I could have reached out and raked my nails along the floor!

The last Hork-Bajir heard my wheels screeching. He looked back over his shoulder.

WHAM!

Flying Hork-Bajir! I caught him in the tail and legs. He went flying. Up, a cartwheel, over the top of me as I raced beneath. I saw him hit the ground in my rearview mirror.

Cool?

Way cool!

WHAM!

Another Hork-Bajir. This one sprawled into a small mountain of bags of Doritos, Fritos, and Tostitos.

Now the others had realized I was on their tail. They scattered. Left and right. Left, through an automated test of coffee machines. Right, through a quiet, turned-off test of canned cheese.

The bright glitter of the silverware drew me. I yanked the wheel, spun completely around, yelling with glee as I did, straightened out, fishtailed, and roared after one big Hork-Bajir.

WHAM! Bu-Bump!

I caught him a glancing blow. He fell and managed to get his arm under my back wheels as I rolled on.

It was the most fun I've ever had. I mean, if there's a heaven it must be a lot like this.

Ahead, a new target! No, wait, a knot of targets, all with their backs to me.

Hork-Bajir! Human-Controllers! And three big, ugly Taxxons, all surging into one corner.

I hit the brakes. The car fishtailed to a stop.

I heard the bellowed, harsh language of the Hork-Bajir. I heard the cries of humans. I heard the slithery speech of the Taxxons. And above it all, the roar that made grown men wet themselves: the roar of the tiger.

I had found Jake and the others.

I climbed out of the car. The upholstery was seriously damaged. Maybe the BRI should test that.

I surveyed the scene, not wanting to miss a single, glorious detail.

Perhaps as many as fifteen Hork-Bajir. Four humans. Three Taxxons. Versus a tiger, a gorilla, a wolf, a young Andalite warrior, and a Hork-Bajir that had to be Tobias.

I was fiercely glad for Tobias. He'd managed to get into a seriously dangerous morph in time for battle.

It was a scene of perfect beauty. Blood slicked the concrete. Taxxon guts lay in steaming piles. There were bellows and cries of pain.

Battle! Desperate and deadly!

I almost cried at the sheer loveliness of it.

Then I plowed in.

CHAPTER 15

Nice Rachel

I woke up. Someone had kicked me in the ribs. I didn't have to guess who it was.

She snapped on the light and glared down at me.

She reached down, yanked Bobo Bear out of my arms, and ripped his arms out, sending stuffing flying everywhere.

"Leave Bobo Bear alone!" I cried.

She knelt down over me, menacing. "Don't make me mad. I'm already as mad as I need to be. If you make me any madder I won't be responsible for what happens next. Get me?"

I nodded.

71

She twisted away and threw herself on her back on the bed.

"S-s-s-so, did you have fun?" I asked.

"Fun?!" she shrieked. "FUN?! Did I have FUN?!"

"Hey, get off the phone, Rachel, and stop yelling. Sara's asleep!"

This was from my mom, outside in the hallway.

"Okay, Mom!" I said.

"Your cousin," Mean Rachel whispered, her face twisted with rage.

"Jake?"

"Jake! I should have killed him. What he said to me! To ME!"

"What? What happened?"

"I saved their sorry butts. Oh, man, you would not believe this battle! This one Hork-Bajir caught me with his blade and chopped my left arm off, right? I mean, I'm in grizzly morph, we're totally outnumbered, and this Hork-Bajir gets behind me and SLASH! This sudden pain! Then, thud, and I realize my arm is on the ground. Hah HAH! On the ground. So you know what I do? I reach down, pick it up, and use it like a club to beat him over the head."

I felt like I was going to throw up. "That's awful!"

She looked puzzled. "What's awful?"

"Never mind."

"So we kick butt, right? I mean, we rock and rolled! And we escape! And then Jake goes off on me. On ME! Jake! On ME!"

"Didn't he, you know, didn't he think it was cool when you hit the Hork-Bajir with your arm?"

"He goes off on me with 'You screwed up the plan. You come barreling in here looking for trouble while we're trying to sneak around and find the stupid Anti-Morphing Ray.'"

"Uh-huh."

"I'm trying to be nice. I'm like 'You stupid moron, you were getting your weak little butts kicked. I heard the alarm go off and I saved you. I am a hero.' But he's, like, 'Rachel, *we* set off the fire alarm to draw the Hork-Bajir away. You show up busting in doors and they realize they're under attack.'"

"Well, I guess I can kind of see his . . ."

Her look stopped me dead.

"I mean, Jake is such a moron!"

"Exactly! We kicked Yeerk butt! That's what we do. Forget the stupid Anti-Morphing Ray, who cares? We kicked Yeerk butt!" She shook her head. "Jake has to go."

"Well, I —" I started to say.

"Shut up, I'm tired."

She snapped the light off and within seconds she was breathing deeply.

73

I lay there on the floor, in the dark, holding my armless Bobo Bear.

What was I going to do? How was I going to live with her?

Not that it mattered what I thought, or what I wanted. I mean, I was, like, helpless. She was the one who . . .

I stopped breathing.

Yeah. Yeah. She was the one who would decide what was done.

So, what if she decided she didn't like sharing her life with me?

Would she . . .

Oh my God, I realized. Yes. She would.

CHAPTER 16

Nice Rachel

I went to school. It was comforting, you know? It was familiar. It was safe.

I don't know where Mean Rachel spent the day. I was just glad she wasn't in school. I mean, there are some teachers I don't like, but that doesn't mean I want Mean Rachel throwing them out of the second-floor windows.

Cassie came up to me after English.

"Meeting," she said.

"What?"

"Meeting. After school. You know."

Yes, I did know. The Barn. The Animorphs. Tobias.

Her.

"Or we could go shopping," Cassie said with a bland smile.

I'm sure my face lit up. But then I realized: Cassie hated shopping. And meetings weren't exactly optional.

She was testing me.

"No, we'd better go to the meeting. Right?" I asked anxiously. "I mean, that's what we should do, isn't it?"

"Why?" Cassie asked.

I shrugged. "Everyone will be expecting us. I mean, we have to, right?"

"Yeah. You're right. See you."

Couldn't I just, like, quit? That was the thing to do. That way Mean Rachel wouldn't be all, like, mad?

Besides, I had to meet my dad. He was flying in for just an hour on his way to an assignment in Argentina, and I had to take the bus out to the airport.

Of course I could have just morphed and flown out there. That would be quicker and easier and less expensive.

I imagined that. Imagined flying. Flying was fun. If you didn't think about it too much. But if you want to fly you have to morph. And the idea of my skin turning into feathers and my bones shrinking and my organs going off into Zero-space to be a big blob of blood and skin and assorted body goos, well, that was so totally gross.

A bell rang and I jumped.

"Switch to decaf," Marco said. He was standing right by me. Waiting to go to our next period, which we had together.

"Oh, hi," I said.

"So. Purely hypothetical, here," he whispered. "Mean Rachel goes with Tobias, right? And you think I'm cute, right?"

"What?"

"Come on, we have to get to class. I'm just saying Tobias and Mean Rachel. I mean, that's the way it'll happen, don't you think?"

"Don't you think Tobias likes *me*?"

He shrugged. "How can he like both of you? I mean, you look alike. Very alike. Identical. And may I say I approve of the mini. It's the look for you. I guess what I'm getting at here is, how are you and Mean Rachel going to divide up your lives?"

We were walking down the hall, jostled by kids running past in both directions.

"I don't know," I admitted.

"She's a little intense, huh?"

"Duh!"

"Kind of creepy, really. I guess you wish you had someone you could talk to about it."

"Uh-huh."

"I mean, wow, the psychodrama of it all. It's the ultimate *Jerry Springer.* 'Meet a girl who has been split into two halves, good and evil.' Man, I'd watch."

"Uh-huh."

"But it has to creep you out, right? I mean, no offense, but now you're Rachel but without all the psycho-killer parts of your personality. So you have to be wondering what's going on with your life, right?"

"I guess so. She made me sleep on the floor." I don't know why I told him that. I shouldn't have told him that. It was embarrassing.

I saw his gaze flicker. I saw the smile fade for just a moment.

I stopped walking. "You know I'm not, like, this total moron now, okay? I know you're testing me."

"Testing?" he asked with a mocking laugh.

"Jake told you to check on me. See if I seemed like I was maybe losing it. Right?"

Marco laughed. "We're there."

"Where?"

"Class."

I shouldn't have told him. Marco would tell Jake I was unreliable. He'd tell Jake that I'd probably blurt out anything. And I didn't know if I had fooled Cassie, either.

Of course I hadn't fooled Cassie. No one fooled Cassie.

I fought down the panic that welled up inside me, threatening to choke me!

Had to get out! I had to get away from all this. My . . . my other half was probably already thinking of how to get rid of me. And my friends? Would they try and stop her?

No. I was useless to them.

Useless to the Animorphs, maybe even a danger.

Suddenly school wasn't so comforting.

CHAPTER 17

Mean Rachel

I was early to the barn. Suddenly it occurred to me: I could spy it out! I should have thought about that earlier. Only why bother to load up your brain with a bunch of "what if?" stuff? The future is not my problem. Live for today, fight for today.

I morphed to fly. Not as cool as a big raptor, maybe, but with its own weird powers.

I did it in the barn itself. Why not? No one else was there. They'd just be getting out of the yawn factory.

I stood there, surrounded by creatures of the wild: fierce raccoons, aggressive geese, and rabbits that . . . well, there wasn't much good to say about rabbits.

I focused my mind on the morph.

My skin blackened and crisped. You know, like I'd been burned to overdone marshmallow consistency? Only instead of mushy marshmallow consistency, this was like fingernail.

My body squeezed into three portions. My head was a BB resting atop a muscular abdomen. Below that my waist pinched tight above a growing, swelling thorax.

My arms became sticks. My legs extended out and out, thinner, thinner and yet incredibly strong.

Two new arms burst from my chest.

<Hah HAH!> I laughed gaily. <Let my wimpy twin try this some time. She'd go insane!>

All the while I shrank and shriveled and seemed to fall toward grains of sand that became boulders and pieces of straw the size of felled telephone poles.

Suddenly my blue eyes inflated like balloons. The blue iris turned glittery black. My eyeball itself was shattered into thousands of tiny facets, each a sort of separate eye.

Very cool.

My weak human mouth, pale lips, and blunt, tiny teeth, became the long sucking-tube of the housefly.

81

I tested my wings. I was airborne in an instant. A totally different type of flying than an eagle, of course. An eagle is a killer. A fly? A fly eats dog poop.

Ah well. A hunter, a killer; a soldier must do what a soldier must do.

I flew, wild and bobbly and blown by any stray air current, but I made it to one of the crossbars of a cage. I rested there, waiting.

I didn't have to wait long. But it wasn't my friends who arrived first. It was a boy who seemed, to my fly senses, to be a blurry explosion of weirdly colored light.

Erek. His hologram was not designed to fool the fly's compound eye.

The android looked around, switched off his hologram, and now seemed to be nothing but a pile of steel and ivory. The colors were still off — the fly eye sees the color spectrum differently.

If the Chee was here waiting, he had news. Important news.

Pathetic creature. He had deliberately chosen to resume his pacifist programming. We had freed him to be a warrior of such great power that not even I would ever have challenged him.

And yet, in his moment of glory, having done more destruction in two or three minutes than we had done in months of missions. Having littered the floor and smeared the walls and ceilings with his vanquished foes, he had deliberately chosen to reintegrate the programming that would force him to die rather than cause harm to a living creature.

It bothered me. It was a waste. And . . . and it just bothered me, that's all.

Maybe I'd ask him. Later, not now. Why? Why would he do it?

The Chee's hologram snapped on. The door of the barn opened. Jake led the way. They were all there, huge, blurry, purple-hued beings, shattered into hundreds of images. They spoke in confused vibrations that rattled the spiky hairs on my back. Ax demorphed from human to Andalite. It was like watching a slow-motion explosion at a paint factory, so colorful and weird to my compound eyes.

Tobias flew in through the open loft and rested on a high perch. Time for me to start acting like a fly. Tobias was a hunter! A predator! I had to treat him with respect.

"Erek," Jake said.

"Yes. Trouble. Your raid failed."

"We noticed," Marco said grumpily.

"The Yeerks are moving the Anti-Morphing Ray."

"Where?"

Erek caused his hologram to shake its head. "Don't know. There's a level of secrecy that even we cannot penetrate. All we've learned is that they're moving it. And that they are being very, very careful about keeping it hidden. They'll load the AMR aboard a truck. Three trucks will leave Buyers Research Institute. They'll go three different ways. Only one will have the AMR."

"Three trucks?"

"Three trucks. Three routes," Erek said. He looked around. "Where's Rachel. Or should I say Rachels, plural?"

"I don't know if Crazy Rachel even got the word," Cassie said. "She wasn't in school today."

"Yeah, the total lack of ambulances was proof that she didn't go to class today," Marco said dryly.

"I have to go," Erek said.

"Erek" — it was Cassie — "is something bothering you?"

The android hesitated. "No." Then, "Yeah, I guess so. It's stupid, really, but it's like I'm jealous."

"Of who?" Cassie pressed.

"Of Rachel. The nice one. She's done it, hasn't she? She's found the way to fight a war and suffer none of the pain. She takes all the evil inside her and sends it off on its own to do . . . to do what has to be done. I guess there are times I wish . . . well, forget it."

He shrugged. No one said anything. The Chee left.

<Okay, look,> Tobias said, speaking for the first time. <Before either of the Rachels gets here, we need to talk. We need to figure out what we're going to do about them. I've been talking to Ax. He says maybe — only *maybe* — we can put her back together again.>

CHAPTER 18

Mean Rachel

<We would require enormous amounts of power,> Ax said. <And the two Rachels would have to agree. And there would be a definite possibility that both halves of Rachel would die in the process.>

"Unacceptable," Cassie snapped.

"What *is* acceptable?" Marco asked. "The present arrangement? A pathetic whiner who's made up of all the fear and self-doubt and indecisiveness and airheadedness that hide way down inside of Rachel? Or the psychotic killer, the rage machine that Rachel has managed to keep under control for so long?"

Psychotic? Was Marco saying I was crazy?

Crazy? Why? For wanting to annihilate my ene-mies? For standing up for myself? For taking no bull?

He was going to regret saying that.

"That's not all there is to it," Cassie said. "I think the split goes beyond that. I don't think Mean Rachel is capable of long-term thinking. Nice Rachel is, but she's not capable of short-term focus. Rachel busted in last night with no idea what to do. No plan. She was just reacting. But Nice Rachel laid out a shopping trip yester-day that was like a general planning an inva-sion."

Marco said, "Strategy and tactics. Long-term, short-term."

"We can't use either of the Rachels we have," Jake said.

I began to demorph. I was just beginning to grow when I realized what Jake had said.

Couldn't use me?

Couldn't *use* me?

I'd use them! I'd use them till they cried for mercy!

I was growing fast now. I was sitting atop a gate. The rough-textured wood was receding be-neath me.

<She's here!> Tobias snapped.

At that moment I lost my balance and fell from the gate edge. I fired my wings, but they were already melting. I hit the floor. I was too small to be hurt by the fall and I kept demorphing.

<You're MEAT, Marco!> I shrieked.

"She's out of control," Cassie said sadly.

<Shut up you tree-hugging moron!> I screamed. <I'll take you down, too!>

I was growing, growing! Bigger and bigger. Human first, then I'd morph to . . . but wait. No! I'd made a mistake! In my human form I would be vulnerable.

I *was* vulnerable!

NOOOOO!

"Ax?" Jake said quietly.

I saw huge hooves moving swiftly closer. I knew what would happen! They would kill me while I was weak. They had to! It's what I would do, they had no choice!

<Don't kill me, I didn't mean it!> I wailed.

"No one is going to kill you," Jake said.

<Yes you will. Let me live! I want to live! You can't hurt me. You can't kill me. Weaklings! Fools!>

All the while I was demorphing, growing, becoming more and more human. Although I was still mostly fly when the wimp showed up.

"Aaaaahhhhhhhhh!"

She screamed.

I lunged for Marco.

CHAPTER 19

Nice Rachel

Hideous!

Foul!

It was me. Me! My face with that long, spittle-dripping proboscis where my mouth and nose should be. My body with dwindling stick legs sticking out of my chest. She had grown to nearly human size, but with enlarged fly features still lingering.

I couldn't stop screaming.

"Aaaaahhhhh! Aaaaahhhh! Aaaaahhhhh!"

She . . . it . . . I . . . had her hands around Marco's throat. Ax was trying to swat her with the flat of his tail but she'd gotten Marco between her and the Andalite.

89

Mean Rachel struck Marco's face with the open tube end of her proboscis. She used it to cover his mouth and nose, shutting off his air, muffling his own cries of outrage and disgust.

"Aaaaahhhhh! Aaaaahhhhh!" I screamed.

"Rachel, shut up!" Cassie snapped at me. "My parents could come home any minute!"

Marco punched Rachel in the stomach. She swatted him with one of her brittle, stick arms. But she was still becoming more human and there was no great force behind the blow.

Her proboscis shriveled away, clearing Marco to breathe. And allowing her to talk.

"I'm taking over! Who's with me?!" she cried.

Jake took a running jump at her, but Mean Rachel released Marco and dodged aside. Jake hit the floor hard. A flutter of wings and Tobias was dropping from above. He maneuvered in the still air, looking to grab a talonful of blond hair and distract her long enough for —

But Mean Rachel was too quick. She shot an arm straight up, grabbed Tobias by the feathery leg above the talon, yanked him down, and wrapped her free arm around his body.

Then, with perfect malice on her face, she closed her fist around Tobias's neck.

"Mess with me and Bird-boy here is a dead chicken."

Everyone froze.

"Hah HAH!" she crowed. "Too easy! I don't even need to morph!"

<Rachel, what are you doing?!> Tobias yelled, more mad than scared.

"Sorry, my love," she sneered, "but as a predator, you'll understand."

"Okay, everyone chill," Marco said.

"Chill?" Mean Rachel screeched. "You called me 'psychotic'! How can a 'psychotic' person chill?"

"I meant 'psychotic' in a nice way," Marco said.

"I am in charge now!" she cried. "I'm running the Animorphs! I am the boss! You'll all obey me. ME!"

"Whatever you say," Jake said placatingly. He moved gradually closer to her. "You want to be in charge, fine. I'm tired of the responsibility anyway."

"Yeah? Then here's my first order: I want Marco killed! No! Wait. Not killed. He may still be useful."

"Glad to hear that," Marco muttered.

"Don't kill him. Just . . . just . . ." She looked around wildly, frantic, her eyes blazing. "Just punish him. That's it! We'll whip him! Tie him down to that stall door and we'll whip him! Whip him till he screams!"

"Okay," Jake said. Then he shot his right fist

out, past a squirming Tobias, to connect with Mean Rachel's left cheekbone.

"Ax!"

Before Rachel could recover from the shock of the sudden attack, an Andalite tail blade was at her throat. Marco grabbed one arm. Cassie grabbed the other.

Tobias fluttered to the ground, picked himself up, and flew back to the top of the barn.

Mean Rachel began to thrash. To scream.

"Aaarrrgghh! Aaaarrggghh!"

Out of control!

She fell to the floor, writhing, spit flying as she screamed curses and threats which soon were nothing but incoherent roars of rage.

Cassie, Jake, and Ax held her down. To protect themselves. And to protect this mad, rabid beast from injuring herself.

I was crying. Face in my hands, crying.

"She's not me! She's not me!" I wailed. "She was never in me!"

But I knew the truth. My memories were all intact. I knew that this Rachel, this tortured, wild, vicious thing had been a part of me.

She had made me brave. She had made me strong.

Poor, sick, twisted thing, she had made me . . . me.

CHAPTER 20

Mean Rachel

Man, you never saw a bunch of kids so upset over nothing. I mean, I was mad. So what? Who wouldn't be?

Anyway, they let me up after a while, and then Jake decided the meeting was over. And I decided I'd put off any action on the Marco problem till later.

The list was growing: Bailey still had to die. And now Marco. Probably Jake.

But that was okay, there would still be me and Tobias and Cassie and Ax.

Of course Ax was kind of devoted to Jake. And Cassie . . .

I headed home, feeling a little confused. A little weird. Like I kind of didn't know what to do next.

The others would probably never accept me as long as my simpy twin was around. They pretended to like her better.

Of course, in a fight who were they going to turn to? Me. I was a natural leader: strong, violent, determined. I could figure out what to do about the truck convoy.

I could. If I really wanted to.

But when I tried, I realized to my shock that I couldn't. It was strange. Like . . . like when I tried to use that part of my brain, the planning part? No one home.

Was Cassie right?

I tried again. Nothing. Not just like I couldn't come up with a great plan. It was like I couldn't come up with any plan. Couldn't really think ahead like that. Like the future wasn't real, or possible, or . . . it just wasn't there.

I'd done okay at the BRI, hadn't I?

Of course that wasn't planning. That was spur-of-the-moment reacting. Yeah. I could do that. I could react.

Her.

She had that part of me! The rotten little weasel! Wussy Rachel had part of my brain. A part I needed!

I'd have to take it from her! I'd have to . . . How?

It was too complicated. I felt like my brain was going to explode. I got home, shoved past my little sister, and stormed up to my room.

Up till then I'd been okay with the split. I mean, it was like finding out you have this tumor, this tumor of weakness, sickening weakness, growing inside of you. That was Rachel. Wussy Rachel, I mean. A tumor full of fear and indecision, and getting all that out of me was great, great, GREAT! Liberated, man! Free! Yah HAH!

Only . . . she had the part of me that could plan. That was wrapped up in all that fear.

I needed it back. I needed to figure out how to get it back and all I could come up with was: Kill her! But, no. That wouldn't work. Would it?

I stormed around my room ripping the covers from my bed and kicking whatever I found to kick.

Where was she?

I jerked my head left, right, left. Not here. Why not? Where was my other half, the half with part of my brain?

Not here.

I felt suspicion tickle the adrenaline into my bloodstream.

Not here. Plotting against me with my own brain!

My eyes blurred with rage. But then focused again. In purple ink, *purple*! A new note on our desk calender.

I leaped to the desk.

"Call Daddy." Then, separate, "Daddy. Flight 545. Gate 17."

This information worked its way into my feverish brain. I knew instantly that she was going to betray me. Of course! Yeah, if I thought about it, if I strained to remember, I could recall what I'd been before. I had to think about what the old me, the two-sided me, would have thought of doing when she, I, we, were depressed or worried.

Daddy. Of course. Without me to give the stupid fool some backbone . . .

I was morphed in two minutes. I was going to the airport. Yes! That was clear.

And then?

Kill! Yes, kill! Kill!

I wasn't sure who, but I was sure of that much.

CHAPTER 21

Nice Rachel

I was, like, in the restaurant? Having a croissant? I didn't want one, duh, but you had to, like, order? Or they don't let you sit there?

Anyway, I had my croissant, and I told the waitress my dad would want coffee when he got there.

The display board showed flight 545 on time, and the restaurant was right across from his gate. He knew where to meet me.

But he would be totally surprised when he found out why I wanted to talk to him. I mean, it's, like, "Dad? There are these aliens? And they, like, go into your brain and all?"

97

He would freak.

Unless he already knew. Of course he probably wouldn't know unless he was one. A Controller, I mean. That would be really bad.

I'd have to make sure he wasn't. I mean, I like, like, Tobias. I don't want anything bad to happen to him. Or Cassie, who is my best friend forever and ever.

And I owe them . . . something. Yes, I owed them. I had to protect them. Had to be sure.

There was a croissant right in front of me. Why was there a —

"Daddy!" I squealed, catching sight of him. I jumped up and waved. He waved back and came toward me.

He didn't look like a Controller.

Of course, I guess they don't. I guess there's no way to tell.

"Hi, honey," he said. He gave me a kiss and a hug.

"Hi, Daddy."

"Need some coffee."

"I know. I, like, told the waitress, okay?"

The waitress actually remembered and came over with coffee.

"So. What's the emergency?" he asked me.

"What?"

"Well, you kind of implied there was something major. Something you couldn't tell your mom."

I nodded. "That's right. I couldn't tell her because she might be one of them."

"One of what?"

"So could *you.*"

"I could be? What?" he asked.

I looked at him. Very shrewdly. "You tell me."

He shook his head. "Okay, back up. What is it I could be? Or is it your mom?"

He seemed confused. But maybe that was all a ruse. I waved my hand to chase away a fly.

I leaned forward. "Look me right in my eyes and tell me you're not."

"I can't do that unless —"

"That's right, you can't because you don't even know what I'm talking about, do you? Oh, poor Daddy! Poor, poor Daddy, you don't know. But I'm going to tell you. No more secrets, please?"

"Absolutely."

I glanced left and right. I mean, after all the times Jake and Marco reminded us all about keeping secrets, I'm not some idiot.

And something was nagging at me, needling the back of my brain. Couldn't betray the others. I couldn't.

Then, in glancing left and right I saw something frightening.

She glared at me from across the room. From over my dad's shoulder.

I felt like just dissolving.

She jerked her head.

I felt the tears start. "I have to . . . to . . . I have to go to the ladies' room!"

CHAPTER 22

Mean Rachel

The wimp blew past, all tears and snot. I tried to trip her, you know, just for fun, but I missed.

"T'sup?" I demanded of my father, twisting the chair around backward so I could sit astride it.

"What's up?" my father said. He looked closely at me. "Did you just change clothes?"

"Yeah. Leotard. Big thing now."

"Are you barefoot?"

"Hey, I see why you're a reporter. You're a regular genius."

"Rachel, have you joined some kind of a cult?"

"Yeah. The Cult of Me!" I laughed. "What, is there NO service in this dump? Where's the waitress? Get over here and wait on me! On ME!"

My dad put his hand on my arm. I flashed on the silverware. It'd be funny to see how fast he could yank that hand back after I planted a fork in it!

"Sweetheart? The waitress is busy with —"

"Stop waiting on that ugly old woman and get over here!" I yelled. "The strong should be served before the weak!" I pounded my fist on the table to emphasize this fairly obvious point.

"Rachel! Stop it. Now!" my father rapped.

Okay, now he was gonna get the butter knife. Only . . . there were people all around. Not now. Later.

"You're on my list," I said with a contemptuous sneer.

"I don't know what's gotten into you!"

"It's what's gotten *out*!" I said and roared with laughter.

"Sweetie, listen to me, I don't have much time. It's just a connecting flight. You need to tell me what's bothering you."

"Right now? You."

He hung his head. "Okay, look, I know I've missed a weekend or two. But I've been really, really busy. You know I love you."

"Bet you don't anymore," I said and guffawed again at my wit.

Suddenly, to my amazement, I spotted the wimp. She was actually edging back. Not right for the table, more like she was going to circle around behind me and . . . but why?

I had to think it through. Why? Okay, she would circle around behind me. Then . . . kill me?

"Listen, Rachel, I am still your daddy, even though I —"

"Shut up, I'm trying to think!"

If the wimp kept moving around till she was behind me, well, um . . . my dad would see her!

That was it! My dad would see her!

A plan! I had to stop her!

Oh . . . oh . . . what? What? I —

"FOOD FIGHT!" I screamed. I jumped up on my chair and pitched a croissant speedball at the next table.

No one joined in.

My dad grabbed my arm and dragged me away. I'd have to kill him for that. But for now, it was working. The wimp was left behind.

Ten minutes later my dad was on his plane, and I had left.

"Nice try, Wonder Wuss," I sneered at my nitwit double.

CHAPTER 23

Nice Rachel

I was trapped!

Mean Rachel had cut me off from my father. I had nowhere to turn. I could go to my mom, sure, but we've never really shared our secrets and all.

Not that she's not a good mother. She is. We just don't have that whole spill-your-guts thing going on.

Spill your guts! What a horrible phrase.

Anyway, I went to see Cassie. But she was on her way to meet up with the others.

I'd forgotten. There was going to be a mission.

Tonight!

"Don't worry, Rachel," she said. "I don't think Jake will want you to come along."

We were in the barn. Cassie was administering medicine to a raccoon with an infected leg.

"Oh, good," I said with relief. "Because it sounds dangerous. You know?"

"Yeah, I know."

Tobias was the next to arrive.

"Hi, um, Tobias," I said.

<Hi.>

Nothing else. Just "hi." I was getting the feeling I wasn't all that welcome among my friends. Not even Cassie or Tobias liked me.

"Are you guys mad at me?" I asked.

"Mad? No, of course not. It's just . . . you know. You're different."

"But I'm better," I said. "I mean, I'm, like, nice. I'm not all crazy."

<We're used to crazy,> Tobias said. <I mean, who else would, you know, care about someone like me? It takes a fairly crazy girl to like a Bird-boy.>

"You like her better?" I asked in total amazement.

"Her? Oh, you mean Evil Rachel?" Cassie laughed. "No. She's insane and dangerous. I just want old Rachel back. No offense."

"But, you can't expect me to ever want her back inside me, can you?" I asked.

No answer, because right then Jake came in with Marco, and Ax in his human morph.

They looked wary.

"What do we have here?" Marco asked Cassie.

"Wimp Rachel," she said. Then winced. "Sorry."

"Oh fine, if you all like her so much, I guess I'll just go home!" I pouted. "Only . . . it's getting dark out. Can someone walk me home?"

Jake rubbed his head like his hair was annoying him. "Rachel, look, we need you."

<We do?> Tobias wondered.

"And, Mean Rachel, I assume you're here in some morph spying on us, so you can hear this, too," he said. "Look, we have this convoy thing. Three trucks. Three directions. If we eliminate both Rachels that leaves us with five people for three trucks. Meaning that someone is on their own. I don't like that. Everyone needs backup."

<I would not require backup,> Ax said. He had morphed back to Andalite. I had looked away.

"Even you need someone to give you some cover, Ax," Jake said. "I'm sorry, but this has 'trap' written all over it. If the Yeerks are being this careful, it's because they're worried. Which means they could be waiting for us. We need six people, minimum."

Marco backed him up by holding up six fingers. "The question is, who is number six? The psycho killer or Baby Spice, here."

"I can't go!" I cried in horror.

"Yes, you can," Cassie said firmly.

"I would have to morph!"

<You have morphed hundreds of times,> Ax pointed out. <Although you have been altered, your memories are apparently intact. Can you not draw on those memories for courage?>

"No."

<She said no,> a new voice said.

It was Mean Rachel, of course. Jake had been right: She was hiding, in morph. Something hideous was growing inside one of the empty stalls. It looked like someone had taken a Barbie doll and a Beast Wars Transformer and melted them together in the microwave.

Jake instantly began to morph to tiger. Ax moved toward her, tail ready. Marco, too, began to change.

By the time Mean Rachel was fully human, she was facing a tiger, a gorilla, and a very alert Andalite.

Only Cassie stayed human.

Mean Rachel looked around and burst out in a loud guffaw. "Got you all scared, haven't I? Come on, fight fair, at least. I'll take on any one of you. I morph to grizzly and we go at it."

<You would lose,> Ax said confidently.

Mean Rachel seemed to consider that for a moment. Then she got a crafty look on her face. "You know what the wimp tried to do today?"

<Yes,> Tobias said.

That startled Mean Rachel. "What?"

"We watched you both," Cassie said. "I was close by at the airport. The fly you waved off, Nice Rachel. Tobias watched you on the way there and back."

Mean Rachel's lips were white with growing rage. "You all think you're smart? You think you can handle ME?"

Jake moved with liquid feline grace over to stand in front of her. <Let me remind you of something, Rachel. We've been through this before. David had morphing powers and he attacked the group. He's a *nothlit* now, trapped in the body of a rat on that godforsaken little pimple of rock out in the ocean.>

"I'm not David!" Mean Rachel spat.

Marco answered, <No, you're not. David might have been able to forge an alliance with the Yeerks. You can't. The Yeerks believe in control. And you are out of control.>

"I can fight! *She* can't!" Mean Rachel yelled, sticking a quivering finger in my face. "She's useless!"

<No, you are useless,> Tobias said. <You're

nothing but rage and violence. You're a pile of gunpowder, ready to go off with any spark. You blow up.>

"I blow up Yeerks!"

<Gunpowder is only really dangerous when it's confined, controlled, used in the right way at the right time,> Jake said.

"I am going on this mission!" Mean Rachel screamed. "You can't stop me!"

She lunged at Jake. She attacked him with bare hands. Jake ignored her assault. He waited, while she punched and clawed and pounded on his head and shoulders. Occasionally he would deign to block a blow with one of his lightning-quick paws.

At last Mean Rachel sat down, spent. Burned out.

<Bare-handed, you attack a tiger,> Jake said. <That's why you aren't going.>

"I *am* going," she said weakly.

<No.> Jake turned his orange and black face to me. <*You* are.>

"No way!"

<Not to fight. Just as backup. Just to run and find the others if I get into trouble. You'll have to morph, but you won't have to fight. I know you don't like it. But, Nice Rachel, *you* are going.>

"Why do I have to go?" I wailed.

<Because. It's your duty.>

109

"My duty?" I thought about the word. Duty? What was duty? What did that mean to me? Nothing!

Only . . . it did mean something. To my surprise, it did. It was kind of weird. But down inside me, untouched by the split, I felt the word resonate.

Mean Rachel got the courage. I got the sense of duty.

And now that I had touched that part of me, it seemed powerful. Irresistible.

"Okay, now that was just, like, totally bad planning," I muttered under my breath.

CHAPTER 24

Nice Rachel

"If she goes, I go," Mean Rachel yelled.

<Okay,> Jake relented.

Mean Rachel looked happy. Until Ax slapped her on the side of her head with the flat of his tail.

Then she just looked unconscious.

"We can't restrain her," Cassie said, looking down at my double. "She has all our powers. We can't exactly tie her up."

<No,> Jake agreed. <And she may come after us. If she does . . . if she *does*, assume that she is an enemy.>

<Great,> Marco said. <The Yeerks ahead,

111

Mean Rachel behind. This should be fun. If by "fun" you mean terrifying and insane.>

Cassie looked thoughtfully at me and smiled. "I told Jake I thought your sense of duty was part of this half of you."

"And I thought you were my friend."

Marco and Jake were demorphing. I forced myself not to look away. It was hideous, horrifying, but I tried not to look away.

I wasn't brave. I wasn't. But Cassie, as usual, was right. Jake had touched something still alive and strong inside me: duty.

Stupid word! Stupid idea!

No, not a stupid idea. But definitely a stupid word. I mean, it sounds like "doody." I mean, puh-leeze. I had to go and get killed because of something that sounds like you're talking about what dogs do on the lawn?

"Okay, here's the plan," Jake said. "Ax with Cassie. Marco and Tobias. Me and Rachel."

Of course. Jake didn't trust me, duh. He wanted me with him so he could watch me.

"We assemble in the air over BRI. The Chee have been alerted to take our place at our homes."

Marco groaned. "I hate it when we do that. The Chee who plays me always cleans my room. I can never find anything!"

"We stay on alert till we see the trucks move

out. One member of each team demorphs each half hour. That way we all stay fresh and don't have time limit problems. Questions?"

Marco held up his hand. "If I split into two halves can I stay home?"

Everyone laughed. That nervous laugh we all have when we know Marco's just trying to ease the tension.

It would take more than that to ease my tension. I felt like I must be as stiff as an ironing board. I knew what was coming.

"Okay, let's morph," Jake said.

He winked at me. It was supposed to make me feel confident. It didn't.

I closed my eyes tight. Owl. That was the right morph for flying at night. Everyone knew it. Owl. They weren't too scary. Not too scary. Not too scary.

I squinched my eyes as closed as I could. And I let it start.

I saw nothing. And, of course, there was no pain. I mean, if you could, like, really *feel* morphing it would be beyond any pain. It would be like burning alive while being put through a garbage disposal or something.

So I didn't feel it, not in that way. But I felt parts of it. Faraway, like when you go to the dentist and they give you Novocain and it doesn't exactly hurt, only you know it should, because, like, they're drilling into your teeth, so it kind of does hurt?

That's what morphing is like.

And you can hear it, too. You can hear your bones crunching and grinding as they shrink and twist and hollow out. You can hear your skull as it changes shape and you think, *Oh! Oh! My brain is being squished!*

And you feel yourself totter, off balance, as your body changes shapes and your feet become hard, scrabbly talons, and when you wave your arms around to keep from falling you feel the extra resistance because now you have, like, feathers?

But through it all, I kept my eyes shut.

<Rachel? You're done,> Cassie said kindly.

I opened my eyes.

<Yah!> I yelped in surprise. Owl vision, of course. Too, too much. I closed my eyes. Then, slowly, peeked again.

<You okay?> Tobias asked me.

<Noooo,> I wailed.

<Let's fly,> Jake said.

Duty. Stupid, stupid word.

Nice Rachel

It wasn't that flying isn't cool. It is cool. I mean, parts of it. Like being able to see everything from up in the air. That was kind of interesting.

But here's the thing about flying? You're up in the air!

There is nothing holding you up but air. Nothing. You're a hundred feet up, or whatever, and in your head you're still a human, still looking at the world like a human, still thinking "Oh. My. GAWD! I'm up in the air!"

I mean, if you lean out of the window on the third floor of a building it scares you, right? Even though you know most of your body is still inside the building. Well, when you're flying, it's not just three stories up and there is no building and if you start falling you're going to have a lot of time to scream and think about it before you hit the ground and smash every bone in your body.

<You okay?> Cassie asked me.

<Nnn-hnnn,> I said.

We flew through the night. The six of us. The Animorphs. We'd done it . . . I'd done it a hundred times, probably. I remembered all those times. I remembered flying to some mission or other and being filled with anticipation.

I used to look forward to it. The fighting. The missions.

And yet, when I thought back on it now, it wasn't all Mean Rachel. I was there, too. I'd been scared. It wasn't that I wasn't scared. It was just that Mean Rachel had gotten us past it. She'd made us brave, with a mixture of courage and recklessness and desperation and insecurity.

And there had been insanity, too. Something down deep inside that was dark and hard and cruel.

I wondered about the others, my friends. If they had been split like this, what would they have become? Did Jake have a Mean Jake inside him? Oh, yes. Definitely. And Ax. Neither of them might be as wild or out of control, but they had that same core of darkness.

Cassie? No. Or at least a split-screen Cassie would be this huge portion of nice and this tiny bit of rotten.

As for Tobias? He flew, still his own hawk self, a little above, and a little apart from all of us.

If you split Tobias into halves you'd have what you already had: a hawk, and a boy.

It was okay to think about all that. It took my mind off what was coming.

Which was?

Oh, yeah. Following some trucks.

Well, maybe that wouldn't be so bad. I mean, I was already morphed. I was already flying. All we'd have to do is fly above the trucks.

<There's BRI,> Jake said. <Okay, separate. We don't want to look like an owl convention.>

For a while after that we just floated in the air. Me and Jake stayed close together, mostly. He didn't ask me how I was doing. Probably he didn't want to know.

Then . . .

<They're on the move!> Marco reported. <Doors opening. Three trucks visible inside the building.>

<Okay, everyone get set,> Jake ordered. <Left to right we call them trucks number one, two, three. Ax and Cassie, truck number one. Marco and Tobias? Number two. Rachel? You stay on my

117

wing. We have truck number three. As soon as our truck clears the building we intercept and try to land.>

<Land?> I asked shrilly.

<On the truck.>

<Excuse me? I thought we were, like, *following* them?>

<Rachel, an owl cannot keep up with a truck that may go sixty miles an hour.>

<So . . . so . . . NO!>

<Rachel, we need you.>

<NOOOOOO!>

The trucks began to move, big, lurching boxes below us and a couple of hundred feet ahead. Jake slanted down in an intercept dive.

I hesitated.

Duty.

Doody.

I let the air spill from my wings and dove after him.

CHAPTER 26

Nice Rachel

Down, down, down. Faster, faster, faster. And all in the most eerie silence. Owl wings make not a whisper.

The truck, blazingly bright to my owl eyes, grew closer fast.

We were going to crash into it!

No, we were going to shoot past it and hit the ground!

No, we were going to hit short and slide under the huge wheels!

<Aaaaahhhhhh!> I cried. <I'm scared! I'm scared! I'm scared!>

<Me, too,> Jake grated. <Just stay on my

119

wing. Don't think. Get out of yourself, pretend you're somewhere else.>

<What? What? I'm an owl on a collision course with a truck!>

<Let the owl do the flying, Rachel. It's just like swooping down on a mouse. See that strap that goes across the top of the truck?>

<Y-y-y-yes.>

<See the overlap? The row of rivets? That's your target. Your mouse. Just let the owl do the flying.>

I tried. I honestly did, but Jake was INSANE!

What did he mean let the owl do the flying? We were ten seconds from impact. Nine. Eight.

And then, to my amazement, the owl took over. It was so weird! It was like one second I was in the cockpit of a plane and I had no idea how to fly it, and then, suddenly, the pilot came in and took over.

I focused on those stupid rivets. I focused and the owl focused and we got closer and closer and closer and . . .

Strike!

Talons grabbed.

Scrabbling, slipping . . .

The truck lurched hard. I lost my grip, rolled over on my back, blown back along the top of the truck's box.

My talons slashed, desperate, looking for a

hold where there was only slick, featureless steel.

<Aaahhhhh!>

Tick!

A talon grabbed! A tiny hole, a screw hole. One nail of one talon snagged in that tiny hole.

I saw Jake, latched on to the strap up ahead of me. The others? All gone, by now.

I wanted to cry. Wanted to just sob and weep and boo hoo. I was shaking. My feathers were quivering. My mind was sinking fast, sinking into dark despair.

<Rachel! Demorph!>

<What?>

<Demorph! Now!>

<Here?> I couldn't be hearing him right. Was he crazy?

<You have to demorph to morph,> he said. <Just listen to me, Rachel. Listen to me. Stop crying, stop freaking out, just listen to me.>

I focused on his thought-speak voice. I tried to shut out everything else.

I began to demorph. Better to be human than owl. Just one problem: my talon. At any moment it might turn into a toe. A toe would not hold on. I would go rolling off the edge of the truck onto the street to be crushed by —

<Rachel! Listen to me. Demorph. Do it!>

<I'm t-t-trying!>

121

I began to change. To grow. I mean, I understood what Jake was going for. I understood that he figured my human skin would help hold me to the steel.

He was right. As skin replaced feathers I began to stick better. I kept my eyes pressed tightly closed.

"Rachel. You're done demorphing," Jake said in his human voice.

"Good," I whispered. The truck swerved. I slapped my hands down on the metal, trying to hold on.

"Okay, now you have to morph again."

"What?"

"Roach. Cockroach."

"No! No way! Never! No no no no no no no . . ."

CHAPTER 27

Nice Rachel

"Rachel!"

"No no no no no . . ."

"Rachel! There's a tunnel up ahead. This truck is too tall. The tunnel is too low. If you're still human when you get there you'll be scraped off."

My mind was reeling. You know, you see that phrase in books: My mind was reeling and you think, *Whoa, what's that about?* But I can tell you: My mind was reeling.

It was totally impossible. I had to choose between being killed by a tunnel, or turning into a cockroach?

What kind of world is it when you have to

make choices like that? A bad world, that's what. Bad, bad, very bad.

"Listen, just close your eyes like before," Jake urged. "Come on, hurry! It's the only way to stay alive."

It did occur to me that maybe Jake was lying. Maybe he was only telling me this in order to get me to do what he wanted. But how could I know? How could I possibly know?

I squeezed my eyes shut and kept myself pressed as closely as I could to the cold steel box of the truck.

Roach? I had done it before. I'd morphed to cockroach lots of times. Lots of times. Nothing to be afraid of. Nothing to worry about.

Except for the fact that I would be turning into a cockroach!

"Eyes closed, Rachel. Eyes closed."

It was so strange. Not the morphing. I mean, yes, the morphing, but that's not what I meant. What was strange was that you know you can be scared of something, then you go ahead and do it, so the next time you're not as scared? Like the fear wears off, becomes weaker?

That's the normal way for things to be. Only it wasn't that way for me. I had now morphed to owl. And I had demorphed. So it should be easier for me now, right? Plus, I'd done it, like, hundreds of times: bear, fly, whale, flea . . . I had all

those memories, perfectly preserved. I knew . . .
I mean, I *knew* that had been me doing all those
things. So why should I be so scared?

But I was. The fear was untouched. Undimin-
ished. Not one iota less powerful. It was like the
part of my brain that was capable of thinking,
Hey, that wasn't really so bad, was just gone.

It was. It was in my twin.

The thought made me very sad. It meant that
I was never going to be able to get brave again.
Never. Like there was some kind of fear-coping
organ and mine had been surgically removed.

I was trembling. Shaking. Teeth chatter-
ing. Until I had no teeth. Until I had no flesh to
tremble.

I was aware that I was shrinking. I could tell
because my palms were dragging across the steel
as hands and feet all became much closer.

But I kept my eyes shut and told myself it
wasn't happening to me. Wasn't me. Someone
else. Not me.

Then, the two legs erupted from my chest.

I yelled. Only I didn't, because now I didn't
have a mouth. I tried to make a yell but I no
longer had lungs. No throat. No vocal chords. No
tongue or lips. All gone!

I screamed in thought-speak.

<It's okay, Rachel. It's okay, Rachel,> Jake
kept saying. <Keep at it. Bridge is coming up.

Hurry. Keep morphing. There's time, but don't stop!>

I kept morphing. Only I wasn't even there anymore. My mind was off, faraway. Off in a warm, cozy place with a big comforter pulled up to my chin and my eyes closed and . . .

The cockroach feelers activated. I was flooded with sensations. Smells! Vibrations!

My eyes weren't closed anymore.

<Good work, Rachel,> Jake said. I guess he said it about a hundred times before, at long last, my panicked mind came floating down to Earth again and I heard him.

<Are we past the bridge, yet?> I whispered.

He didn't answer.

So. He had lied. That's Jake: The mission comes before anything.

I didn't want to see, feel, hear, but I had no choice. Roach sight is almost nonexistent, just vague shapes floating in shadow. But hearing and "smell" were pretty good. And I could not turn them off.

So I was aware that the truck was slowing down now. And I felt it when the truck passed from cool outside air to much, much warmer air.

In the distance I saw a huge, dull glow. And I felt vibrations that my roach brain interpreted as vast, low-pitched sounds.

Then, I felt the difference in pitch as the truck headed downhill.

<Some kind of tunnel,> Jake said, sounding worried.

The truck stopped.

There was a smell . . .

Gas!

<De . . .> Jake said.

And I was gone.

CHAPTER 28

Nice Rachel

I woke up.

I tried to open my eyes. No eyes. No vision.

My antennae brushed something above me, sending a tingle through my body.

I was in roach morph!

Oh, God. Oh, God, I was in roach morph!

I ran. Panic. Fired my six legs and ran.

A wall!

Left. RUN!

A wall! I was in a corner.

Turn around. Other way! RUN!

Wall!

NO, no, no! Not walls. A box! I was in a box!

In a box! An inch taller than me, an inch wider, an inch longer. A box! Trapped!

<Rachel, try and stay calm,> Jake said.

Demorph! I screamed to myself. *Demorph!*

I began to change, to grow, but instantly I felt the awful, unyielding pressure. Walls all around me!

<Don't demorph, you'll die!> Jake yelled.

I could barely stand to listen. I morphed back, but the panic, the terror!

Oh, God, they had me! At long last, they had me! Trapped. As a roach! As a cockroach!

I started screaming. I kept screaming. Screaming and screaming and screaming.

CHAPTER 29

Mean Rachel

My eyes snapped open. I saw rafters. I saw a stall around me. Someone had rolled up a blanket and put it under my head. Another blanket was laid over me.

"Aaarrrgghhh!" I yelled and jerked up off the ground.

I was awake, up, and mad within a split second.

"Knock me out? Knock ME out? I'll kill you! I'll kill you all!"

The animals in their cages shrank back from me. As well they should.

That does it, I thought. *Now they all die! I don't need any of them anymore. Especially not*

130

that simpering, mewling, uptalking nitwit double of mine.

But how to get them? Had to follow them. That was the first thing. Had to follow them. But how? How? I didn't even know how long they'd been gone. I could have been under for minutes or hours.

I slammed outside into the evening air and scanned the sky. A hawk! No, just a crow.

How was I supposed to find them? The lights were on in Cassie's house. Did her parents know she was gone? No. No. Of course not. The Chee. That's how we'd done it in the past. The Chee would send one of their androids over, armed with a hologram that would perfectly duplicate Cassie. So "Cassie" was probably in there right now having dinner.

I was hungry.

I could kill something and eat it!

Focus!

It had been one thing following them to the BRI. I'd been able to see them then. This was harder. How was I supposed to track them through the sky?

Wait, maybe they weren't too far gone, yet. That was it! Take to the air and hope to get lucky! Good plan.

Moments later I was in owl morph and push-ing for all the altitude that low-altitude bird could give me. I scanned the skies ahead, behind, left, right, up, down, NOTHING! Out over the interstate I flew. The car headlights were painful, the taillights lurid. Too bright!

Had to go after them. Had to hunt them down and kill them! Now! Right now! But . . . but I couldn't find them!

<AARRRGGGHH!>

I could feel the rage frenzy coming on. I was losing control. My wings were trembling. My talons were clutching compulsively at the air. I wanted to scream and scream and find something, anything, to kill, kill, KILL!

Then, I spotted the truck. The truck with something that could only be a girl morphing to cockroach.

Nice Rachel! I crowed to myself. *Jake and my twin, both together! Perfect!*

But the truck was moving away at a pretty rapid speed. Too fast for me to catch. All I could do was watch helplessly as it veered down a circular off-ramp, then turned onto a smaller four-lane road.

The turn around the off-ramp gave me a few seconds to play catch-up. But then the truck was off again and pulling away fast. In five minutes it would be out of sight.

Once it was out of sight I would have to think, think about what it had done, think of a plan. No! No, I had to maintain contact. It was the only way.

<NO! NO! I will not be denied my vengeance!> I cried.

Then, at the very limit of my sight I saw brake lights blaze. The truck was slowing. I pushed my wings for all they were worth. I flew as fast as an owl has ever flown. I was practically delirious with the wondrous images that filled my head: Jake and Nice Rachel, both as cockroaches. Hah! Killing them would be almost too easy. I could . . . I could eat them! Yeah, that was it! I could eat them, ah hah hah HAH!

Or maybe I would rip off their legs and leave them helpless on their backs to . . . no, wait. That wouldn't work, would it? But why? Some reason. They . . . I strained my mind, trying to figure out what it was that was bothering me about that scenario.

I pull off their legs. Okay. That was good. Then, I put them on their backs so they can't roll over. And then . . .

I would eat them! Yeah! Swallow them in one big bite!

But even that made me feel uncomfortable. Like I was overlooking something.

Frustration was building now. It was a physical thing, like a pot coming to a boil in my guts. And the more it boiled, the less I could focus, the more it boiled, the less I could focus, the more . . .

<Aaaarrgghh!>

The truck was slowing. Turning down a side road at right angles to me. I could keep up, now! Barely. The truck approached a vast, rusty fantasy of steel. A foundry? Where they made steel or something? Maybe. It glowed a deep orange in the night.

The truck entered a doorway. Gone from sight!

I could eat them. One big bite.

The frustration! I felt like I wanted to claw my own brain open. Not working. My brain was not working. Now, what? And then, what?

<After them! Follow them!>

That was easy enough. Down I went. Catch them. Kill them. Yeah, yeah. That soothed me a little. Don't worry about the details.

Down and down and down. I swept through the huge, open doorway.

CHAPTER 30

Nice Rachel

<No! No! No! No! No!>

<Rachel! Rachel, it's Jake!>

<No! No! No!>

<Rachel, listen to me. Listen to me, Rachel. I know you're scared. I know you're scared, Rachel. Listen to me.>

Moaning. A moaning cry came from deep down inside me. A soundless sound, a voiceless, pitiful mewling. My brain . . . gone. Thinking . . . impossible.

Just terror. Animal terror.

<Listen to me, Rachel. We've been in lots of tough spots, Rachel. Lots of tough spots.>

<Oooooh, ooooh, oooooh.>

135

<Remember when the Yeerks were trying to get to the President and the world leaders at that conference? Remember how we thought we were done for, trapped by, like, a hundred Hork-Bajir?>

<Oooooh, oooooh, ooooooh.>

<We made it, though, right? Or remember when we were dolphins and we were in that fight with the sharks? Or how about the time we . . . come on, Rachel. Hang in there. Hang on.>

<Ooooh, oooooh, ooooh.>

<Okay, look, I can't see much, okay, just like you. But I don't think we're the only ones. I think I see other . . . containers. You know, like the ones we were in. I think what happened is the Yeerks hit the truck with nerve gas and just grabbed everything that fell out. You know? Bugs of whatever kind. Not just us.>

<Oooooh, oooooh, ooooooh.>

<There are Hork-Bajir here, walking around us, I think. Can you tell? Can you look and see, Rachel? I know roach eyes are pretty lame, but see if you can make any sense of the shadows and movements. It may help. Rachel? Rachel?>

I couldn't. Couldn't look. Think. Just scream and scream. Scream. SCREAM! SCREAM! SCREAM!

<Rachel! Stop it, stop it right now!>

I fell silent.

<I'm going to tell you what to do, Rachel, and you are going to do it.>

Silent. Waiting. Feeling the terror stalking me, feeling it tickle up beside me, feeling its cold hand reaching right through me. Trapped! A roach in a clear, plastic matchbox. No way to demorph. No way out. Trapped!

<Listen to me, Rachel, I want you to tell me everything you see. Do it!>

<I-I-I-I see . . . I see . . . shadows. Moving. All around. Tall, huge!>

<Are they Hork-Bajir?>

<Yes. Don't know. Maybe. Yes. Hork-Bajir. Oh, God!>

<Listen to me, Rachel. What else do you see?>

<A light. Red, maybe. A clock, I think! Numbers in red. Counting down. Ooooohhh!> I moaned. I knew why they were counting down.

<Rachel, listen, it's the Yeerks playing mind games. They want us to be scared. It's a countdown to make us think we're running out of time in morph. But listen, Rachel? They aren't even sure we're not just real bugs, okay? They don't know, Rachel. They're hoping. They're guessing. They don't know. Do you understand?>

Counting down. Trapped. The rest of my life as a roach! Not a hawk like Tobias, a cockroach! No! No! NONONONONO!

<Listen to me, Rachel, you can't say anything to them when they come. You can't say anything. No matter how much —>

Say? Say? My feverish mind grabbed on to that thought. I could talk to them! I could beg them to let me go, let me go, let me go.

<Rachel, listen very carefully to me,> Jake said. <You cannot say anything. It's the only way to survive. It's your duty.>

<Help me! Help me!> I began to scream in open thought-speak.

<Rachel, no!>

<Help me! I'll tell you anything, just let me go!>

Suddenly, movement!

They were coming for me! The Hork-Bajir! Yes, they would let me out, let me out and I would tell them anything.

WHAM!

My box was snatched up.

Fwit!

I flew through the air.

Then, *slice*!

I fell through the air.

CHAPTER 31

Mean Rachel

Turned out I didn't need some big plan. I saw Hork-Bajir, I morphed to Hork-Bajir and joined them. Hah! All I had to do was march along like they told me.

The room was gloomy, lit only by faint, greenish luminescence that seemed to glow from the walls.

There were a dozen pedestals. On each pedestal a small, glass box. And in each glass box a bug or other small animal. Roach, ant, snail, beetle, fly. Weird. Like some kind of insane collector had gone to a lot of trouble to capture and display some rare animals that were not at all rare.

One thing was for sure: Jake and my idiot twin were two of those bugs. And they were dead meat!

I laughed. Silently, of course. The Yeerks thought *they* were going to kill Jake and the other Rachel. Hah! I was going to kill them! No one was going to deprive me of that.

I was in Hork-Bajir morph. Not any different than the other three Hork-Bajir in the claustrophobic little room. Except that those three didn't know who I was. They didn't know what danger they were in.

Me against three? I had the benefit of surprise. Besides, I was me. ME!

"Boring, huh?" I said to a big old Hork-Bajir beside me.

He glared at me. Probably a little thrown off by my use of correct English. Hork-Bajir mouths and brains don't handle English all that well, so they use a mix of languages: their own, and ours, and Yeerkish, of course, and *Galard,* and I didn't care, because he was eyeballing me, and I was enjoying the moment of suspense, the point where time slowed down to a crawl as I prepared to attack!

He said something about how it wouldn't be boring once Visser Three arrived, and as soon as he'd garbled out the last word, I struck!

Right wrist blade to his throat!

Ah HAH!

He slumped, looking surprised.

The second Hork-Bajir just stood there, puzzled, but number three was a smart Yeerk. He knew right away. He leaped at me. Too late!

I had a foot up, cocked, as I leaned my weight back on my tail, waited for him to rush me, STRIKE!

"RrrrAAAARRRGG!" he bellowed in pain.

<Figure it out, yet, genius?> I said in thought-speak as I mocked the slow one. And then I swung. But even though he was dumb as dirt, he was quick. He dodged. I slammed into a pedestal and knocked it, like a domino, into more pedestals that fell over, sending their little bug boxes skittering.

The Hork-Bajir who I'd gut-taloned was up, holding his insides with one hand and fumbling for an alarm switch with the other.

BrrrrrEEEEET! BrrrrrEEEEET!

The dumb one lunged. Dug an elbow into me! I windmilled my arm, tore his blade loose, and slammed the side of his head with my own head.

He didn't drop. I didn't drop. And now it was one-on-one mayhem!

Slash!

Slash!

Hork-Bajir blood was flying!

<Ah hah hah HAH!> I cried in sheer pleasure.

BrrrrEEEEET! BrrrrEEEET!

Old Gut-rip had definitely set off the alarm. And now the doomed fool was throwing the stupid bug boxes at me! Hah!

Slash! Slash! Slash! Slash!

Four bug boxes, four sliced in half by my supernaturally fast blades.

My main antagonist saw this and worried. He hesitated.

<Come on, Yeerk, let's dance,> I crowed.

He lunged. I lunged.

Crunch. I heard the sound of a bug squashed beneath my foot. I could only hope it wasn't Jake or Rachel. I wanted them to *know* I'd killed them.

Slash! I ducked. Swiped up, caught my foe beneath the chin.

Bye-bye chin!

Three of them! I'd taken three of them down! I was a goddess. Nothing could stop me! No one! Invincible!

And now, to find Jake and the pitiful creature who called herself Rachel.

Suddenly, whooosh! The wall behind me slid up. Gut-rip staggered out. Out into a much brighter room beyond.

A dozen more Hork-Bajir waited, vibrating

with destructive energy. And in the middle of them, the one, the only, the most dangerous creature I had ever fought.

Visser Three.

<Close it, you fool! You'll let them escape!> he shouted in a deafening thought-speak roar. I saw his Andalite tail whip and catch Gut-rip with the blade that was sharper than any Hork-Bajir blade.

The wall slammed down.

<Well, well,> he said, more calmly. <I had my doubts that we'd caught an Andalite. But now, I doubt no more.>

<Come on in!> I yelled. <Come in here and I'll kill you!>

<Yes, you might,> he said smugly. <So I think I'll have to decline. Instead, I think I'll simply wait. Call me when you are ready to submit to me, Andalite.>

<Submit? I'll cut your heart out!>

<No, I don't think you will. See, I have an Andalite body. I control an Andalite mind. And I know how to break you. Oh, yes, I do.>

I heard a strange sound. Sliding. Slipping.

I looked up. It was hard at first to tell in the dim light, but then I realized it was true: The ceiling was coming nearer and nearer. And one wall was closing in as well.

<Is there anything an Andalite fears more

143

than being slowly, inexorably, crushed?> Visser Three said softly. <Is there anything a free-running, herd animal like you fears more?>

<I'll kill you!> I roared. <I'll kill you!>

<When the room begins to squeeze the air from your lungs, call for me, Andalite. Call for me.>

CHAPTER 32

Nice Rachel

I was on the floor! Out of the box!

Huge, Hork-Bajir feet stomped all around me. But then, after a while, all was quiet. All but the sound of my twin's thought-speak voice raging at Visser Three.

Then, the terrible realization of Visser Three's threat: that I had escaped one box only to find myself trapped in another.

Demorph! I told myself. But, no, morphing was horrible. And Rachel . . . the other Rachel . . . might kill me. She had to be furious.

What should I do? I was trapped, unable to decide. To demorph was terrifying, to stay in morph was terrifying. It was the ultimate horror

145

of the coward: I was caught between two frightening choices.

Logically if both choices were terrifying, then it didn't matter. But it did! There was more at stake than fear. I had to find a way out! I had to survive!

Demorph, Rachel, you idiot! I berated myself. *You pathetic coward.* It was true. Without my other half, what was I? Someone too scared and weak to save myself, someone who could be trapped, helpless, paralyzed between alternatives.

The demorphing began. I don't even know when I started. I just did. And slowly, then more quickly, I began to emerge, to grow, to feel flesh on my returning bones.

"You," Mean Rachel grunted in disgust.

She had demorphed. She was human again.

"I came here to kill you. You and Jake," she said. "But as you can see, we have other problems."

She jerked her head up at the ceiling. It was slowly descending. The back wall was simultaneously moving forward. It would have been impossible in a normal room. But the Yeerks had the technology.

"J-J-Jake?" I managed to stammer as my lips and tongue and throat formed out of roach shell.

She shrugged. "Who knows. I stepped on a bug. Maybe that was him."

"Oh, my God!" I wailed.

"It's a war, he was a warrior, warriors die," Mean Rachel said dismissively. "The important thing is I'm in charge now."

"We shouldn't be human," I said softly, crying hot tears for Jake. "Visser Three . . ."

"I don't think he can see in here," she said. But she was doubtful. Obviously the thought had just occurred to her. But still, she was probably right. If Visser Three had visual contact with us he'd have come in by now, seeing us as humans. Mean Rachel was right. By accident.

"I'm gonna morph to grizzly bear," Mean Rachel said. "I'll kick butt!"

"But the walls are closing in," I moaned. "If you get bigger you'll just get squashed sooner."

She looked up at the ceiling. She bit her lip. Soon, very soon, there wouldn't be room for a bear. Soon after that there wouldn't be room for a human.

"If he wants to kill us, why doesn't he just kill us?" Mean Rachel demanded.

"He doesn't want to kill us," I said. I was sitting, eyes closed, hands over my head.

"Of course he wants to kill us, moron!"

"No. He wants our bodies. Only not *our* bodies. He thinks we're Andalites. He wants us to surrender. Wants to break us so we'll let him take our Andalite bodies to use as hosts for Yeerks."

I could feel Mean Rachel staring at me. I cracked one eye to look at her. She was troubled.

"Yeah. That's it," she admitted. She hesitated. She looked like she was fighting something inside her own head. Then, "So . . . so what do we do?"

Both my eyes opened. Mean Rachel was asking me what to do? Asking me? Me?

"I'd kill them, but I can't get at them!" she yelled.

I was amazed. It was insane. Mean Rachel, psycho-killer Rachel was asking me what to do. But when I even tried to think about it I couldn't. I mean, I could, but I couldn't think about me doing anything.

I could see possibilities: The Visser thought there was only one of us. He wanted us alive. I could see possibilities, plans. But not for me!

However, I *could* think of Mean Rachel doing them.

CHAPTER 33

Mean Rachel

<You lose, Visser,> the nitwit said, trying hard to sound like me. You know, brave.

<You're the one in a box, Andalite.>

Nice Rachel laughed with a mixture of defiance and fear. The fear was real.

<These Hork-Bajir blades are wonderfully useful, almost as useful as our own Andalite tail blades.>

<Do you think you can slice your way out?> Visser Three mocked.

<No. I think I can slice my own throat.>

The reaction was instantaneous.

Swoosh!

The wall slid out of view. Through my compound fly eyes I could see thousands of tiny images of heavily armed Hork-Bajir. Thousands of images translated as dozens of actual Hork-Bajir. All were poised, ready.

So was Visser Three.

I felt the shudder of fear pass through my twin's Hork-Bajir morph. I fired my wings.

<Make this easy for yourself,> Visser Three urged. <Before you could die from self-inflicted wounds, I'd have surgeons repairing the wound. And if you try and fight your way out we will overpower you with sheer numbers. Surrender, brave Andalite. I have won. You have lost.>

I flew. I flew as only a fly can fly: wild, rolling, jerking, drifting, but ultimately with weird precision.

It was hard to make out the Visser visually in the shattered glass world of my compound eyes. But I could smell the difference between the Andalite body he had and the surrounding Hork-Bajir.

I zipped like a rocket with a busted fin. I landed on a vertical surface. In shadow. And I crawled toward darkness on my six, tiny fly legs.

<Give up,> Visser Three said.

<I . . . I . . . I . . .> my gutless twin mumbled.

I was in far enough. <Visser,> I said. <Oh, Visser Three?>

His head jerked. It knocked me loose from the blue hair I'd been clinging to. I fought the fly's instinct to escape, escape, escape! I stayed within the shadow.

<There's a second one!> Visser Three hissed.

<Yeah. And guess where I am, Visser?>

He hesitated. <Come out and show yourself and I won't have you killed.>

<Visser? I'm in your ear, Visser. Way down inside your head. I can practically see the real you, the Yeerk slug. And here's the thing you need to think about, Visser: What happens when a morphed Andalite the size of a fly demorphs inside your head?>

<You'd die!> he yelled.

<So would you,> I said.

There was a silence that lasted at least two full minutes.

<You!> he roared for no reason. Then more minutes of silence. Then, I felt his body slump, go limp.

<What do you want?> he said at last.

<What *do* we want?> I asked Nice Rachel in private thought-speak. <I forget this part.>

<We just want safe passage outside. No guards. Once we're outside, you'll fly out of his ear. After all, you don't want to commit suicide, right? So he'll believe you.>

I relayed this to Visser Three. Five minutes

151

later, we were outside, in the fresh night air. I flew out of his ear.

The Visser backed away. We backed away.

<Next time I'll simply kill you. I won't take chances. I'll just kill you.>

<Likewise,> I said.

I flew, Nice Rachel ran, and we put distance between ourselves and the foundry. She collapsed in a mess of tears and sobs — weird coming from a Hork-Bajir — when we reached a patch of shabby woods.

<I have to demorph, okay?> she cried. <Then you can kill me if you want.>

I was already demorphing. Soon we were just two identical girls, both named Rachel.

"Poor Jake. I can't believe . . ." Nice Rachel boo-hooed.

<I'm fine,> a voice said.

Nice Rachel jerked like someone had stuck a power line in her nose. "Jake?"

<Who else?>

I saw what looked like a cockroach demorphing. Nice Rachel looked away, the gutless simp.

<That's why I like roach morph,> Jake said. <Hard to kill. I was stuck to the bottom of Mean Rachel's foot for a while. Then I limped over onto Nice Rachel.>

"What, were you just too scared to let us know

you were alive? We could have used some help back there! I'll kill you for that!"

"I wanted the two of you to find a way out," Jake said calmly as he became more human than roach. "You had to figure out that you need each other."

I barked out a laugh. "Me need *her*? Her? The wimp? The wuss? The simp? The mall-crawling nitwit?"

"Yes," Jake said, almost fully human. "You had no plan, no clue. She came up with the plan. She's the one with the ability to think long-term. Without her you're nothing but rage and violence and yeah, courage."

"Rage is all you need!" I protested.

"Nice Rachel?" Jake said, turning to the twit.

She nodded. "Yes. I know. I *do* need her. I can't . . . I can't do anything without her. I know she's crazy, but, you know, she makes me be able to be, like, strong and all."

"Of course *you* need *me*!" I yelled. "I'm me! But you? You're just you!"

"Mean Rachel," Jake said. "Without her, you're out of the Animorphs. Period. You can't join the Yeerks. You can't fight them alone. You want to be a warrior? You need to be able to plan, to have a healthy capacity for fear, and, by the way, a sense of duty."

"Doody," Nice Rachel said and giggled.

"Look, Ax has a plan. Both of you have to go along, or it won't work. May not work anyway. But Mean Rachel, if it wasn't for her, your other half, you'd have lost back there. She saved you, and you saved her, and you're both just huge pains in all our butts the way you are now, so do it, do it, just do it, or I swear I'll give you both to Visser Three."

CHAPTER 34

Nice Rachel

It was the barn. We were all there. None of the others had been ambushed. Their trucks had all been decoys.

The Anti-Morphing Ray had not been destroyed.

Tobias was perched in the rafters, silent, watching with his intense hawk eyes.

Erek the Chee was there, too. I did not know why. Perhaps he was, like, curious?

<You may begin at any time,> Ax said.

I looked at her. At the face that was identical to mine. At the eyes that were so different, so hot and wild and dangerous. She scared me.

155

I reached a trembling hand to lightly touch her bare shoulder.

Mean Rachel rolled her eyes. "If this doesn't work, you're dead, Ax. Dead! Do you hear me?"

Mean Rachel looked at me with contempt in her half-smile. Then she reached for my shoulder and gripped it hard.

"Do you, Dr. Jekyll, take Ms. Hyde, to have and to hold —"

"Shut up, Marco, you're already on my list!" Mean Rachel snapped.

<You must begin the acquisition at the same time,> Ax instructed.

"Count of three," Cassie said. "One . . . two . . . *three*!"

I began to acquire my twin. Her DNA flowed into me, as mine flowed into her. I felt the soft listlessness of the acquiring trance.

Would this really work? I was acquiring her, she me, but I didn't feel any less like myself.

<Erek,> Ax said.

Erek moved swiftly, smoothly. He dropped his hologram and appeared as the slightly canine-looking android we knew as the real Erek.

He placed one hand on me, one on Mean Rachel. Suddenly, I had a bad feeling about this.

"Sorry," Erek said. Then . . .

"AAAAARRRRGGGHHH!"

The pain was indescribable! Both halves of

me twitched and jerked and seized. Every nerve ending exploded with energy. I couldn't hear. Couldn't think. My eyes were blinded by a sizzling halo of light.

<Morph!> Ax yelled in my head. <Morph into the other! Do it!>

Insane! I was being electrocuted! No way could I . . . and yet . . . the strangest . . . strange . . . melting . . . warmth . . . impossible . . .

I fell to my knees. The assault of electrons was over. I could see dirty hay. I could see the feet of the others.

I tried to stand up. Too shaky. Cassie and Jake helped me up.

"Sorry about that," Erek said. "Ax said you needed a massive jolt of energy, and we didn't think you'd tolerate it voluntarily."

I nodded, confused. I looked around. *She* was gone.

No, not gone.

"Are you okay?" Cassie asked.

Okay? I wanted to cry. I was me again. For whatever that was worth. The coward was in me. The killer, too. Human and animal.

"Rachel, do you want to sit down? Maybe talk?" Cassie asked.

"I . . . I don't know . . ." I said.

"I'm here for you," Cassie said.

I looked up. Tobias. Half-human, half-predator. Our eyes met. "Thanks, Cassie," I whispered. "But . . . Tobias?"

<Yeah. Let's go, Rachel,> he said. <The two of you and the two of me. Let's go.>

The darkness was complete.

Total.

And I heard nothing. No sound save my own irregular breathing.

Sensation started to return and I realized I'd been stuffed into a box half my size. A straight-jacket that pinned my wings against my body. Jammed the vestigial Andalite tail up into my neck.

The hawk in me tensed every muscle. No room! In a panic, it pressed against the walls of the seamless box. Terrified. Confined. I fought to control the bird. But I was losing the struggle. The human me was frightened, too.

Rachel! Oh, Rachel. Could she escape this underground network? Somehow survive?

She would. Sure she would. She had to. She was Rachel, after all. Rachel!

Where was she? All I could think of was a par-alyzed fly, helpless and vulnerable on the floor.

Someone would step on her. She wouldn't be able to get out of the way, and someone would kill her.

Better than the alternative. Life as a fly. Trapped, like me. But so not like me. I could see, soar . . .

And the plan? Rachel was supposed to have seen where they took me, then lead the others in. First prove the Anti-Morphing Ray didn't work, then, in the rescue, destroy the thing for good measure.

It was crazy! Inconceivable arrogance on our part. We had underestimated our foe. A fatal error.

Fatal.

The hawk brain, the animal part that still, even now, lived apart from me, untouched by human reason, began a low, defeated moan. A death moan.

So hot in the box. Like an oven. Warmer, and warmer still. How much oxygen could there be? Were they trying to suffocate me? Was that it?

Interminable!

The only external input were the wobbles and bobs as the holder of the box hit me against his leg. The ride continued.

No space to morph or demorph.

<I'll be trapped. As a horrific half-morphed creature,> I pronounced slowly. <That will be my

fate. I bet Andalites don't even have a word for that tragedy.>

That's it. Keep talking, Tobias. Keep talking. Stay sane. Hold on. Don't think . . .

Zeeewoooozeeewooo.

All six walls of the box began to buzz. Vibrate. And then: Poosh!

Like a camera flash, steel walls vaporized. Dazzling light flooded my eyes. Blinded me. Rods and cones shot to hell. I saw nothing but white.

I blinked a few times. Then, no. No, my eyes were adjusting.

I was in another box. But a completely different kind. A cube of glass. Larger, maybe four feet square. Big enough for me to move about. Brightly illuminated, with several spotlights directed at me. I demorphed immediately. Back to hawk.

I blinked again. And as I rose to my feet, I realized I was suspended. The cube hung in the center of a much larger room. I strained to look beyond the glass. Though the glare from the lights to the dimness beyond.

"There's no way out." It was Taylor's voice. Sub-Visser Fifty-one. Cold and casual. "There's no point in looking around."

She sat alone at a long table. Near the door of the large, gloomy, windowless room. To her right and left, armed Hork-Bajir, standing at attention. Above, a network of steel beams and conduits, a daunting maze of wire.

"You may as well demorph and make yourself comfortable while we wait," she continued.

Nice try, I thought. *Demorph and make myself comfortable. Yeah, right! Wouldn't she just love an Andalite to infest. That would get her noticed by the Visser. Why don't I plunge my head in that sludgy Yeerk pool while I'm at it?*

"No?" she prodded, mocking. "Don't want to demorph? Worried about that whole Yeerk-in-the-head thing? That's okay, my little Andalite birdie. You stay just the way you are. For now."

I looked again at the glass walls of my cube. Smooth and thick. Flawless. Featureless, except for one small, inset panel. In the panel were three circles. Three discs like oversized elevator buttons. They were colored. One red, one blue, one black.

"Ah, I see you've noticed the control device. There's a little experiment to be carried out as soon as Visser Three arrives," she said knowingly. "This device is state of the art, Andalite. The very latest in Yeerk technology."

A little experiment? Control device? The Anti-Morphing Ray. That had to be it, right?

I reached forward with my beak to touch the panel.

Scheewack! Kewwwack! Force-field static crackled and hissed. An electric jolt grabbed my beak and sent a shock through my body. From wings to tail and back again. I collapsed, stunned, to the floor.

"Ouchie," Taylor said.